AF322719

THE DREAD SOUTH
BLACKJACK MOONSHINE
SIRIUS

BLACKJACK

MOONSHINE

SIRIUS

BLACKJACK ★ MOONSHINE

A DREAD SOUTH NOVELLA

SIRIUS

THE LAUGHING MAN HOUSE PUBLISHING

This book is a work of fiction. References to real people, events, establishments, organizations, or locales are intended only to provide a sense of authenticity, and are used to advance the fictional narrative. All other characters, and all incidents and dialogue, are drawn from the author's imagination and are not to be construed as real.

Blackjack + Moonshine

www.uncrownednovel.com

Cover Design by Vic Nuckowska

Interior Illustrations by gloomyinks, "Slick as the Devil" illustration by Danny Rivera

Edited by Janus

Royalty-Free images sourced by Pixabay

PRAISE FOR
BLACKJACK ★ MOONSHINE

"A gorgeous testament to the power of horror and of erotic storytelling...Five 'Hell is empty, and all the sexy devils are here' stars!"

Sierra Simone
author of *Priest* and *Salt Kiss*

"...a humid, horrific and sexy southern gothic romp that's sure to leave you thirsty for more than just root beer..."

Wendy Dalrymple
author of *White Ibis*

"...the southern gothic story I didn't know I'd been waiting for. Raw, gritty, visceral, Blackjack + Moonshine is Sirius' best work to date..."

Ravven White
author of *Haunted Hallways*

"...a queer, southern, spookshow romp that'll leave the reader at Bee and Jessie's heels with every shadowy turn."

Kayli Scholz
author of *Saint Grit*

"...*Hellraiser* on ecstasy."

Red Lagoe
author of *In Excess of Dark* and *Impulses of a Necrotic Heart*

For Janus
For reading even when it's gross.

And for Ellis
You foul, slick-tongued devil.

ALSO BY SIRIUS

The Draonir Saga
Uncrowned
Partitioned
Condemned
Disinherited*

The Draonir Saga: Iconoclasts
Hawthorne: A Draonir Novella
The Red Star Society
Admiral Blood*

The Gentlemen Demon Series
Swallow You Whole
Sever Your Spine*

The Wire Killers Novellas
Birdeater

The Dread South Series
Rising Sun Over the Devil's Nest*
Blackjack + Moonshine
Funny Little Town*
Gospel of the Cuckoo*

*2024

CHAPTER ONE

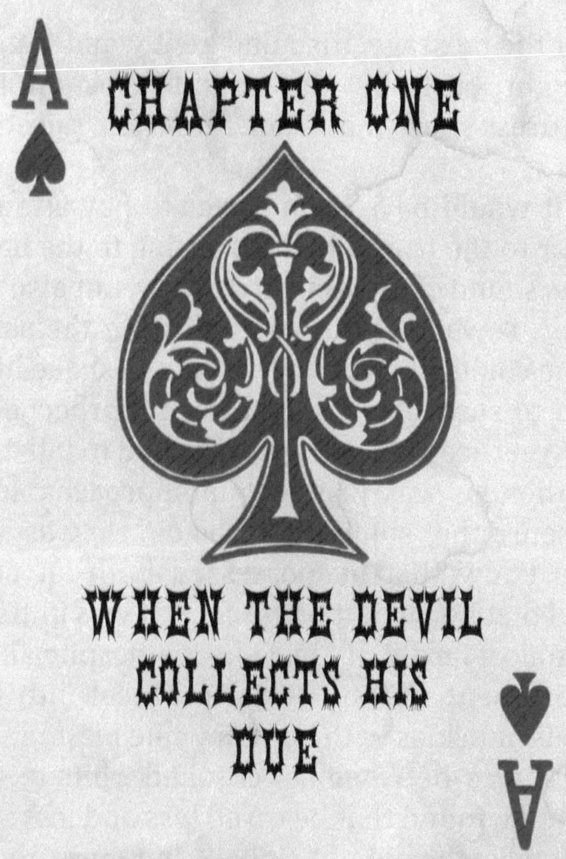

WHEN THE DEVIL COLLECTS HIS DUE

It was damp inside the old church. Three window air conditioning units and five or six whirring pedestal fans were not nearly enough to combat the brutal summer heat. It was the sort of church where you sweated out your sin, paying penance in damp suit linings and itchy black tights while listening to the rhythmic *whoosh* of round silk hand fans that swung through the air as steadily as the pendulum of a grandfather clock. Time disappeared once the dented front door closed and the preacher started talking. All Jessie could think about was how the man at the pulpit looked redder than a tomato and ready to split. All he could smell was the cheap, mildewing blue carpet that had been ground down by a decades' worth of heels to the point where it was almost as smooth as tile. He wasn't even sure about the message. His mind kept wandering and was only brought back by the sound of stomping slick-bottomed dress shoes that made the whole raised platform shake.

Maybe it would have been easier to pay attention if he were closer to the front. He liked sitting in the back row—close to the sound equipment, ironically, but also right next to the door. It was easy to dart out once the service was over and he could avoid anyone trying to shake his hand or invite him to stay after for lukewarm barbecue and jaw-achingly sweet-iced tea. No one had tried to talk to him in a while—either he was just that unapproachable, or they could all sense that something was *off*. He was self-aware enough to know that he possessed both an unpleasant nature and that he wore it on his face. It was impossible for Jessie to smile if he did not feel like it—despite all the years his mother spent drilling social protocol into his brain, swatting his knuckles with her fan while hissing something like *'fix your face'* between her crooked white teeth.

Recently, he found that he cared less and less about how people felt when he did not smile—and more about how it made him feel when he had to push a disingenuous expression to the surface. It always made him feel *wrong*—like his smile was a hair floating at the top of someone's drink. Unwelcome, out of place, and for all intents and purposes repulsive.

And it probably did not help that he was queerer than a pansy bloom pinned to the lapel of a mint-green suit. They could all tell—he didn't need the devil's imprint to know that. They caught on to his wobbling voice and the sparse hairs on his chin, wiry and dark but not enough to bother shaving. They noticed his slim fingers, even though he tried to hide them under gloves—which seemed to only make it worse. Their antipathy was always delivered by sneering smiles from the women and stone-cold looks from the men who stood with their hands crossed over their groins like their dicks were unholstered pistols.

Jessie didn't attend church for the company, anyway. He wasn't even there for the message. He came because he was stalling—because when he got home, he knew that Bee would be there. That slick-tongued fiend with his shiny black cards and his hypnotic hands. Jessie spent a great deal of time clinging to the vain hope that if he lingered long enough, Bee would get bored with waiting and go find something else to do. It never worked that way, but it did not stop him from trying. The devil always came to collect his due—and it was not *only* Sunday, but it was *always* Sunday.

'Insanity is doing the same thing over and over again and expecting a different result.' The thought ran through Jessie's head as he pushed his blunt fingernail against his bottom lip. Four seconds later, he thought, *'that isn't what makes you insane.'*

He was hot. That had to be his problem. Jessie hadn't realized how much he was perspiring until he went to adjust his tie and felt his shirt collar sticking to his neck. The preacher was winding down and the middle-aged woman bent over a keyboard began to play a few chords. That was usually his sign to get out. Jessie grabbed his wide-brimmed black hat from the spot beside him in the pew and pressed it against his chest as he stood. He kept his head bowed to draw as little attention to himself as possible while he slipped out. He could feel a few pairs of eyes following him, but no one reached out to stop him. No one ever did.

It was hotter outside, but less muggy. Jessie closed the door behind him and gulped down a breath of stale, still air that was completely free of department store perfume and unwrapped peppermints. He hoped for a breeze like he hoped for most things—without a single expectation of things working out in his favor. His hat, at least, was enough to keep the sun off his nose as he turned towards the long, winding dirt road that would take him home.

It was only a mile back to his house, and he did not mind the walk. The worst part always came only a few steps in. Catty-cornered to the church was a thick metal post that probably once held a sign, but now it just acted as a bare, silent sentinel presiding over the crossroads. The road that crossed his path was a little wider and more even, stretching out towards the horizon and vanishing past a scattering of dark trees that looked miles away from across the flat grassland.

When Jessie first met Bee, the devil had been standing at that very pole, as flashy and fresh as if he had just stepped off a plane from Vegas. He wore a white suit and a lavender button-up with the first few buttons left undone, and a sleek bolo tie in the shape of a death's head hawkmoth hung loose around his neck. The metal piece rested right against his bare collarbone just at the edge of where his dark chest hair stopped. He shot Jessie a smile full of straight pearly-white teeth, interrupted only by a singular gold canine that glinted with a little spark of life all its own.

The devil's blue eyes were eclipsed by a pair of round purple sunglasses and when he spoke, his words slipped fast through his teeth like a heated televangelist.

'Don't go home, Jessie,' the devil had said without even asking his name. *'There isn't any point in killing yourself when there is no one around to grieve.'*

Jessie had been drawn to him on sight, and then his words hit like a gunshot to the gut. In that moment he stood frozen at the crossroads, teetering on the proverbial edge of awe and terror. Of all the questions that raced along the inside of his skull, the one that stood out in bold red letters came springing off his tongue, *'how did you know?'*

'You set two new razors on the bathroom counter this morning, didn't you?' The devil had a smile that kept growing, like he was grinning at some private joke. *'Those won't do you any good. Let's have lunch, instead.'*

There are those who will talk about being wined and dined by the devil before being seduced into a binding contract and giving up their immortal souls. For Jessie, it had been nothing so grand. They cut a deal over fountain Coke and maple pecan pie under the soft pink neon lights of a diner counter.

Bee seemed to think it was funny, at the time, that Jessie thought he could fill a bathtub with his own blood and fall asleep forever. Bee thought everything was funny.

'You worry too much about nothing at all,' he had said once. *'I can fix all your problems with the turn of a card.'*

Jessie dragged his hand down his face and ground his fingertips against the sides of his brow, as if somehow, that would allow him to push out the anxiety tightening like a rubber band at the top of his spine. He made a sharp turn down the neighborhood street that led to the cul-de-sac where his house rested. It was the only pink house in the neighborhood—and he admittedly liked the siding much better after having it painted. Before then, the whole structure had looked a bit shabby—and on his to-do list was having the roof patched and then getting the windows replaced, once he had the money. After that, the place might just be deemed livable. The yard was a little overgrown, but the path to his door was clear, ending in mismatched bricks that had started to pull up from the soil where they were laid. He reached into his pocket to dig out his keys, though he only had two—the rest of the jingling was from all the keychains he had accumulated over the past year.

The porch swing creaked and he could hear it from the steps. Jessie's heart skipped a beat and he looked up, expecting to see Bee sitting on the rectangular floral cushion with his legs crossed, waiting.

But there was no one. The swing had just been jostled by the breeze and the chains that held it up were in desperate need of oiling. Jessie wiped at his forehead again and found his house key. His hands were trembling a little bit, but he attributed that to the fact that he had not eaten any breakfast.

He spared one last glance behind him before stepping over the flimsy threshold and into the air conditioning. No one was coming. He let the screen door slam behind him.

In spite of how much work it needed, he was grateful for his small house. Jessie could not begrudge the place its 1970's brown carpeting or the overwhelming amount of wood paneling on some of the walls. What was not wood was smoke-stained crème-colored wallpaper with small blue flowers that looked like berries, lined up like soldiers in perfectly straight rows that never seemed to end. The kitchens and bathrooms were filled with yellow linoleum that peeled up something fierce, and all the windows were covered in three layers of sheer, faint white or yellow curtains that were just enough to block out most of the sunlight. He liked his house cool and dark. And considering he had only been in residence for under a year, it could have been worse. The move from Dallas had been a difficult one.

Linoleum crackled as Jessie entered the kitchen. He shed his suit jacket, still warm from the sun, and threw it over the back of a wooden chair. His hat came next, and he ran his fingers through his mop of unruly black curls. His hair was damp from the walk and now that he was inside, he could smell his own sweat. A wave of revulsion drove his thoughts towards a shower. Once he retrieved a cold bottle of root beer from the fridge, all bets would be off.

"I brought you maple donuts." Bee's voice startled him enough that he almost tore the handle off the refrigerator door. "I know that they are your favorite."

Jessie placed a hand against his chest, trying to settle his racing heart as it slammed into his ribs. "Christ," he muttered, "don't you *knock?*" He grabbed his root beer from the fridge and nudged the door shut with his hip.

"Don't swear." Bee flashed a smile. "I also brought blueberry."

"I'm not hungry." Jessie twisted the metal cap off his bottle. "I ate at the thing this morning. At church."

"Oh, are we going back to church, now?" Bee rolled his eyes behind his purple sunglasses. "Sorry, but your immortal soul already has a claim ticket."

"It has nothing to do with my soul," Jessie snipped. "I'm there for the company."

"Certainly," Bee said. "I'm sure they're all fascinating people." He tipped open the box with the use of one finger and offered a glimpse inside. Six maple donuts with soft brown glaze cozied up to six blueberry donuts that were already sweating off flakes of white icing.

Jessie caught hint of the smell and it made his stomach clench, but he didn't budge. "I don't know why you bring them. You don't like sweets."

"But you do." Bee spread his legs and patted his thigh. "Come here. I want to talk."

Jessie fought the sudden, desperate need to obey. He clenched the kitchen counter to anchor himself for a few more seconds while he drank his root beer halfway down. He tried to savor it, but it tasted like nothing on his tongue. It was always like that, with Bee. He had a way of sucking the joy out of everywhere he didn't want you to feel it. Jessie knew that if he went for one of the donuts, it would be the best thing he'd had all day, and he could eat them all in one sitting if the devil didn't stop him. With the root beer, he was using it as a device to disobey, so Bee made sure he didn't enjoy a drop.

That was another thing, things just *were* around him, whether they made sense or not. Jessie set the bottle down with the intention of returning to it later. Even warm, he might be allowed to taste it if he buckled and did as he was told.

Jessie wiped his hand across his mouth, a dirty habit that Bee hated—but also a nervous compulsion he couldn't squash. He walked over to where Bee was sitting and straddled his lap, lowering himself down and resting his arms on the devil's broad shoulders. Bee's hand snaked around and he grabbed Jessie's ass, taking hold of a generous handful and giving it a hard squeeze.

Jessie suppressed a whine. "What do you want to talk about?"

"Well," Bee used his grip to adjust Jessie's position on his lap until he was satisfied. "Have you ever been on a plane?"

"No," Jessie said. He could feel how hard Bee was through his slacks. As much as he resented the fine print of their bargain, his body betrayed him every time. Bee put off heat like a brazier, and feeling his warmth—along with his thick, barely-restrained length—Jessie was already starting to get wet.

Bee knew it, too, he always knew. He dipped his fingers down and teased the taut cross point seam of Jessie's slacks, dragging his nail over the woven fabric.

"Well, tonight will be a first, then," Bee said. "Our plane leaves tonight."

Jessie tried to swallow another whimper, less successfully. "What?" A flare of irritation was not enough to dry him up, especially not with Bee's fingers working back and forth, working him up artfully through layers of fabric.

"Tonight? Did it occur to you that I might—" his breath hitched, "—have plans?"

"Yes," Bee said. He dragged the zipper down Jessie's fly and unbuttoned his slacks with one hand. He worked them down Jessie's narrow hips and slid his fingertips through one leg of Jessie's briefs, pulling them to the side. "And when I checked your schedule, it looked like your plans were to get on a plane and go to New Orleans with me."

"New Orleans—?" Jessie gasped again as he felt Bee push his fingers inside his wet cunt. He clenched his teeth and ground down on Bee's hand, tightening his grip on the devil's shoulders. "Fuck! Why?"

"Why not?" Bee pressed his mouth to Jessie's throat and kissed down the pulsing vein until he reached the collar of his dress shirt. "Come here." He pulled him up a little higher. "Unbutton me."

Jessie did as he was told, reaching down to unbutton the top of Bee's white slacks. Bee used the opening to pull his cock free, and it was only a minute before Jessie felt the hot, heavy tip stroking his entrance.

Jessie pushed his face into Bee's neck and sucked down a hard, shaky breath. Bee's cologne smelled woodsy and sweet, a feral blend of almond and dark amber. Jessie thought about saying something else, something bitter, but any words were cut off when Bee's cock pierced him without warning—crashing through like a battering ram. Jessie made a startled, strangled sound and clamped his thighs down around Bee's. He straightened his back until it arched only slightly, and Bee ran one hand up the curve, pushing it underneath Jessie's dress shirt so that Jessie could feel the heat of his touch. Bee used his free hand to move Jessie's hips how he liked, giving enough force and guidance that Jessie did not have to move at all; he simply had to let himself be used. Bee's cock was thick, and it made him feel like he was being stretched beyond his limits.

Every thrust made him feel like he was being speared, like he was going to split apart at any moment. Jessie wrapped his fingers up in Bee's white suit jacket and clung to him, growling against his skin, inhaling his perfume and riding his cock as if his life hung in the balance.

Jessie placed his mouth against Bee's throat. He took a mouthful of tender white flesh and sucked on it—as if he could ever leave a bruise. He had tried, so many times, to leave as many marks on the devil as the devil did on him—but it never worked. Just one indelible purple mark—that was all he wanted. Jessie bit down, still holding onto Bee's jacket. The pressure made his teeth ache, but he kept biting. He heard something pop and he started to taste blood, but whether it was the devil's or his own, he couldn't be sure. It gushed down his throat and he swallowed, unwilling to release his hold. Bee hissed and he used both hands to grip Jessie's thighs, spreading them farther apart. His efforts were met with the resistance of Jessie's slacks, and he kept pulling. Jessie heard his slacks rip, and then his legs were free. The devil gripped him hard enough to bruise and held him tight against his body, pulling his cock back and then plunging it back in, over and over again until white spots clouded Jessie's vision. Jessie sank his teeth even deeper into the devil's throat, determined to rip out a piece if he could.

"I think I will finish you before you can finish me," Bee's voice was slightly strained, but amused.

Jessie growled. Bee smacked his ass twice, making sure to hit both cheeks before slipping his fingers underneath. He fingertips slid over Jessie's wet clit, working until each gliding stroke was timed perfectly with every thrust. As soon as Bee touched him, Jessie knew it was over. He held on for as long as he could, but with the devil—it always happened fast. Jessie's orgasm slammed into him with the force of a freight train and his whole body shivered as he came. He clenched around the devil's cock and cried out, moaning furiously into the open wound he had created on Bee's throat. Bee's cock pulsed inside of him, and in a few quick strokes, he filled Jessie with his will—there was enough of it that it spilled out before he even had a chance to pull back, coating Jessie's thighs.

Jessie let out a rough, hard gasp and pulled back. His jaw was sore and there was blood all over his chin. Now that he was out of the moment, the taste filled his nose and mouth, coating the back of his tongue. Jessie had tasted blood before. He knew what it was supposed to be—bitter, like pennies—but Bee's blood tasted nothing like that. It was sweet, like red licorice, only the best damn red licorice Jessie had ever tasted.

Bee *wanted* him to like the taste, so he made it irresistible. Jessie wiped his hand over his mouth, just to irritate him.

Bee patted Jessie's thigh and pushed him off his lap. Jessie staggered back a step, leaning over to rest his hand on top of the table as he tried to get his bearings. His legs shook and his clothes were in tatters. He could only imagine what he looked like, with his dress slacks and briefs in two pieces, resting against the floor.

Meanwhile, there was not a single mark left on Bee—no wound on his neck, not even a spot of blood on his white suit. He was pristine. Impeccable, as always.

Bee swiped his thumb over his bottom lip. His gold ring glinted cheekily in the dim light.

"So," he said. "Focus. New Orleans."

He pulled the name over his lips with a near-perfect Southern drawl.

"Tonight?" Jessie managed to ask, despite the fact that he could hardly breathe. "I need to pack."

"No, you don't," Bee said. "We will take care of that when we get there. Although," he flicked his eyes up and down

Jessie's form, adjusting his sunglasses on his nose. "You should change. You are looking a little...run through."

CHAPTER TWO

DRAWING FROM THE FIENDISH BLACK DECK

The following hours were obscured by a Dramamine haze. The last thing Jessie remembered clearly was getting into the passenger seat of Bee's sleek red car and popping two of the round white pills into his mouth. He watched the trees go by too fast as he ground the pills down with his back teeth. He washed the bitter orange flavor out with a swig from a fresh root beer. After that, he could only vaguely recall the lights of the airport—more numerous than the stars—and that sanitized, deliriously stale airport smell. Bee was so *alive* in comparison to everyone there— bodies slumped over in their seats, wrapped in sweaters and blankets with their heads cushioned on flat neck pillows. Jessie trailed behind him, staggering a little from either exhaustion or the drugs, he could not tell. Bee passed him two more pills before to take before they boarded the plane, and beyond that, Jessie didn't remember a goddamn thing.

Louisiana air was like trying to breathe face-down in a bowl of hot soup. Texas heat was dry, and its misery came from the dust and stagnant air. Jessie felt like he had stepped into the shower with his clothes on, turned on the water, and then stepped outside without toweling off. He deeply regretted his choice to wear jeans.

They had no luggage, which might have aroused suspicion in some of the airport employees—except suspicion rolled off Bee's shoulders like water off a duck's wings. All he had to do was flash that infectious smile and it worked as well as a badge; a smile that said *'of course, I have the authorization to do as I please.'* At worst, they treated him like an eccentric millionaire.

No one ever spared Jessie a second glance. Behind Bee, he was just an accessory—as innocuous as a rolling suitcase.

The cottage that Bee had reserved was small and a bit out-of-the-way for being so near the French Quarter. The bright yellow paint made it stand out from behind a short hackberry tree, although up close it was obvious that the pale blue door and shutters were peeling. Inside it was clean—or at least an effort had been made. Jessie knew he shouldn't have been surprised by the fact that Bee booked a place with only one bedroom and only one bed—but it still gave him pause.

"One bed?" he asked.

"Economical," Bee said. "You always talk about how I'm spending too much money."

"Right," Jessie replied. "Although money doesn't mean anything to you, right? You're always saying that."

"Well, which is it?" Bee sat down on the edge of the bed, pushing his hands up and down on the mattress so that the springs crackled. "Men who can't make up their mind aren't attractive, Jessie."

"Or they're just your type," Jessie muttered. He sat down on the other side of the bed and leaned against the headboard. The bed was a double—so not very big. The quilt on top was thin, and a white canopy of mosquito netting was tied up overhead. "Historical."

"A touch, here and there," Bee said. "This place isn't what it used to be." He dashed his tongue over his teeth, as if mulling over a memory before turning his attention back to Jessie. "Are you ready to go shopping?"

"I guess there's no point in hoping you would let me nap," Jessie said. Not that he was very comfortable, but the idea of getting up and going back out into the heat was significantly less appealing.

"You slept the whole way here," Bee said. "Don't be dull." He reached over and squeezed Jessie's leg. "We are going out tonight, and you are *not* going to be seen with me like that."

"Do I embarrass you?" Jessie sat up and rubbed the back of his neck. "What does the devil have to be embarrassed about? You've probably been seen with worse."

"Yes. You look like I found you under a tree." Bee grabbed the underside of Jessie's knee. "Up. I made an appointment."

"An appointment?" Jessie slid his legs off the side of the bed.

"Yes." Bee fixed the cuffs of his lavender dress shirt. "We are going to buy you a suit."

Before Bee, the closest Jessie had ever come to a casino was watching re-runs of old poker games that played on the TV at his favorite bar. He didn't think it would be so loud—or so bright, but bright in a way that there was not quite enough overhead light and a lot of flashing neon from the slot machines. The bulbs that *were* screwed in overhead were yellow and they made the room feel dusky, hazy—like it was smothered in smoke, even though it wasn't. Trust Bee, of course, to find the busiest one.

Bee was not there to play cards. He was there because there were lots of desperate, hungry people he could bat around like a cat with yarn. They all turned their heads when he walked in, not like they could help it. He looked the part of any other tourist, for sure, in his flashy red suit with a gold cross necklace dangling cheekily from around his throat. Even to Jessie, their reactions were almost palpable in the air. Bee had a way of bringing out the worst in everyone. Jessie could feel a pulse of fear, quick and hot—the main emotion they all shared that dominated the room. Jessie noted the people who squirmed in their seats and crossed their legs, as well as those who turned their heads and averted their eyes as if they had something to hide. Bags were drawn closer. Toes curled through the peepshow windows of nylon heels.

Jessie's own chest was tight, but he knew that it was just the beginning. It was going to be a long night. When Bee was like this, every emotion Jessie ever felt was ramped up to a ten. If there was anger, if there was jealousy, if there was fear or lust...Bee would find it. He would pull every lukewarm thought out of Jessie's head on a string and make him feel like it was his last day on earth.

"Hit that blackjack table." Bee nodded towards the opposite side of the room. "Keep going until you're all out." He pressed a wad of folded bills into Jessie's hand.

The stack was as thick as his finger and full of fifty-dollar bills. Jessie couldn't remember the last time he had his hands on so much. Even though it was Bee, and Jessie knew that he could pull money from his deck as easily as he could an ace of spades, it was still enough to take him aback. When he didn't move quickly enough, Bee shot him an annoyed look. The devil lowered his sunglasses to peer over the rims, and just the sight of those blue eyes was enough to make Jessie feel a little lightheaded.

"Until I run out?" Jessie repeated it back to show he had been listening.

"Or they throw you out." Bee slipped his glasses back up his nose and winked. "I'll catch up to you soon."

The crowd swallowed him up like smoke disappearing into the air. Jessie slid the cash into his pocket and rubbed his nose. He would do what he was told, but he hated it when Bee made it so obvious that he was setting him up for failure.

"I ran out." Jessie found Bee. Hours later and the devil still had not caught up to him as promised. Go figure.

"Did you win at all?" Bee was sitting on a barstool and sipping on a mixed drink that was the same deep red as his suit. Jessie could smell the vile mixture of vodka and grenadine from where he was standing.

"One round," Jessie said. "The rest were a bust." He grabbed a stool next to Bee. He misjudged how slick the seats were and how little traction his slacks had. He nearly went sailing backward and had to grab the bar to keep from falling on his ass.

"That is the way it goes. You win some, you lose most." Bee used two fingers to point across the bar. Jessie's eyes followed the gesture but couldn't tell what he was supposed to be seeing. "Look at that," Bee commanded. Jessie expelled a huff.

"What am I looking at?" he asked, leaning one arm against the bar.

"A pair of ladies." Bee smiled, sucking his drink up through its straw until the red was more than halfway down. "Newlyweds, from what it sounds like. Do you want to guess what they are saying to me?"

"No," Jessie said, "but I'm sure you will tell me anyway."

"The one on the left is saying that her ex-girlfriend is visiting town. She is going to go see her tonight after her wife passes out from all the rum. The one on the right is thinking about the mortgage that is due tomorrow. She thinks they are spending too much money here."

"She is probably right." Jessie slumped a little lower against the bar. "Bet you can't guess what is on *my* mind."

"I could split open your skull and lick your thoughts from the fragments." Bee slipped his glasses up into his hair. "You are thinking about food."

"Bingo," Jessie said dryly. "I am starving."

"Well, we don't have any money," Bee said gleefully. "We will simply have to wait until you have earned some of it back."

Jessie furrowed his brow and chewed on the inside of his cheek.

"You are so full of shit," he said.

"I suggest you try the slots." Bee drained the remainder of his glass and set it down on the bar. "You don't need any strategy for those."

"I can win," Jessie said, sitting up. "I'm not an idiot."

"Of course not. But you're not very lucky either, are you?" Bee clasped his hands together. His rings sparkled as they caught the light. "There's another blackjack table over that way. You can try again."

"I'd rather shoot craps." Jessie said as he stood. "Are you coming this time?"

"Of course." Bee set another handful of bills on the bar as a tip. "I wouldn't leave you high and dry."

Jessie cocked a brow but did not say anything further. He slid his hands into his pockets and followed Bee across the casino floor. The ugly patterned carpet squished in places that it shouldn't, while the smell of mildew was barely covered up by the overpowering notes of cheap booze. Jessie was sure that this was the kind of place that cut corners by refilling their top-shelf bottles from the little screwcap liquors out of gas stations. With so much money changing hands, he would have thought they'd spare a little expense to spruce up the place. At least they could gut out the black mold that was too easy to spot crawling in from the water-stained splotches on the ceiling.

They walked by the two women who were sitting close together, the ones that Bee had said were recently married. Bee said nothing as he passed them, but he made sure to catch one of their gazes. The redhead, it looked like—the one sitting on the left. Bee's gaze had a pull, and her eyes followed his until he broke contact. It did not last very long. It was a split-second, at most, but long enough to flip whatever switch Bee had been reaching for. Jessie could see it written all over her face as she turned her attention back towards her partner, mouth open and eyes slightly glazed.

A few more seconds went by, and a screaming argument erupted between them. By that point, Jessie was too far away to hear what was being said—but he saw a couple of men in black shirts that said 'SECURITY' running to break it up.

He was sure that Bee was delighted by that.

A new round was being dealt as they walked up to the table. Bee greeted the dealer like they were old friends and then stepped to the side to watch Jessie play. Bee made a gesture and tugged on his own lapel. Confused, Jessie reached into his jacket. He felt a lump in the little lining pocket and pulled out a folded c-note—one he had apparently 'forgotten about'. He couldn't help but roll his eyes, but he changed it out for chips anyway.

He won the first round. Bee watched intently the entire time, his blue eyes never leaving the dealer's hands. Jessie won again with the second round and then lost the third. If Bee was orchestrating any part of it, he was throwing enough busts for it to seem authentically like a little luck of the devil.

After the fifth round, Jessie was getting irritated. He was up three hundred dollars, and he knew that Bee wanted him to keep going. The money wasn't what mattered, Bee just wanted him to start developing a taste for it. And it was working, that was the worst part.

Winning hit Jessie with a rush he hadn't felt in a long time. It was like going back to his first cigarette or his first sip of whiskey. He wished he had either at the moment—something to distract him from the fact that the combination of lights and noise was causing a massive headache to build up pressure at the top of his skull. Jessie rubbed the back of his neck, hoping that it would help, and threw a look at Bee. The devil did not look back at him, but he stroked his chin and smiled.

"Need something?" Bee asked in his secret way where Jessie could not tell if he had spoken aloud or if the voice was in his head.

"Do they have rum?" Jessie asked, even though there was a fifty-fifty chance he would sound like he was talking to himself.

"Of course they do." Bee was speaking aloud for sure, that time. "Do you want it in a glass or in a bucket?"

Jessie sucked on his teeth. "They give it to you in buckets?"

"Sure do, and they'll mix it with vodka and three kinds of juice until it's a color you can't recognize." Bee flashed his teeth. "And they'll give you a straw wide enough to suck an eyeball through."

"Gross," Jessie said. "What were you drinking at the bar?"

"I don't know. I told the bartender to surprise me. Is that what you want?"

"No." Jessie's teeth hurt just thinking about it. "Just bring me a—hit me." He realized it was his turn, and he looked back at his cards. "Hit me—stand. Do they have anything that doesn't taste like a rocket pop?"

"Do you want *me* to surprise you?" Bee sounded all-too eager for that option.

"How about a vodka cranberry, instead?" Jessie pinched the nape of his neck again. The dealer busted, which meant he was up even more. The sight of the chips getting stacked up so high made his pulse quicken.

Bee brought his hand down on Jessie's shoulder, giving it a squeeze as he walked by. "Double-down on the next bet," he whispered against Jessie's ear. "I won't be far."

"Are you saying I can't win without you?" Jessie hissed back.

Bee chuckled behind him, but did not say anything else.

The sky was pitch black when they left the casino, although the multi-colored lights that filled every window along the street made it seem less dark. Jessie's headache was mostly gone, although he wasn't sure if that was because the bartender had been heavy-handed or because Bee had put something in his drink. Either way, he had downed at least three vodka cranberries and one gin and tonic before walking away from the table. He did not even know how much he had won—he had stopped keeping track. Bee knew. Bee collected the chips at the end and took them to the cage to exchange.

They walked back to the cottage, taking it slow because Jessie kept stumbling into things every time he went over a certain speed. Bee offered him his hand, but Jessie declined it. He took off his suit jacket because it was unbearably hot otherwise and carried it draped over his arm. When they got back, Bee unlocked the door and let it swing open, but he didn't walk inside.

"Get comfortable," Bee said. "I will be right back."

"Where are you going?" Jessie asked, reaching out to grasp the door jamb, already drunkenly working off his shoes.

"To get some food." Bee raised an eyebrow. "You're still hungry, aren't you?"

"Yeah." Jessie kicked off one shoe and it went flying off into a corner. "Hurry back."

"You've got nothing to be afraid of, dear," Bee said. He was gone, then, in a little trail of red smoke. He didn't need to leave the smoke behind. He just liked to.

Jessie shut the door with his foot and started unfastening his white shirt collar. The buttons did not want to cooperate with his fingers, refusing to go through the slim new buttonholes. After a few tries he lost his patience and gripped the shirt by the collar. He ripped it open all the way down to his belt and then pulled it off, tossing it onto the bed. The rest of his suit followed, except for his last shoe— which he had forgotten he was wearing until his slacks got caught on it. Jessie sat down on the edge of the bed and yanked it off, tossing it into another corner—too lightheaded to care if it was the same one as the first.

He found one of the new t-shirts Bee had bought for him and he walked out onto the screened porch, wearing only that and his boxers. There were two green wooden rocking chairs and he collapsed into one of them. The porch light buzzed over his head, barely shedding any light and mostly attracting bugs. The porch looked out into a cluster of trees, so all he could see was darkness and then a little white light from a streetlamp behind them. For a while, the dull roar of cicadas and the occasional rush of a distant passing car was all that he could hear. He rocked his chair back and forth until the headrest smacked against the wall.

'Maybe Bee isn't coming back.' Abandoning Jessie in a city he'd never been in before wouldn't be completely off-base. Bee could have gotten bored and walked off, or he could have decided that the payoff of Jessie's soul wasn't worth his time...there were a hundred reasons Jessie could think of, and he was getting more paranoid as the minutes ticked by. Yet, even if that *was* the case, there was nothing Jessie could have done about it—not at that moment, and he was too tired to get up. He rocked his chair a little harder, taking some satisfaction out of the sound the wood made when it hit the siding.

Eventually, he heard the front door open. Jessie paused, pressing his toes against the porch to stop his rocker from creaking as he strained to listen. He heard the sound of bags rattling, and then a smell hit his nose that was enough to make his mouth water. Jessie's stomach tightened at the scent and his arms suddenly felt weak. He had not realized exactly *how* hungry he was.

"Bee?" he called out, as if it could have been anyone else. There was no response. A few minutes later, Bee came walking out the back door carrying two plates and with one arm looped through the handle of a short metal bucket.

"Careful," Bee said, "it's hot." Even as he gave a warning, he set the plate directly onto Jessie's lap. It was less of a plate, really, more of a bowl—and it burned Jessie's legs through the thin fabric of his boxers. Jessie picked it up immediately, moving it to the glass-top table in front of him that didn't match either of the chairs.

"You figure?" Jessie asked. He couldn't see Bee's smirk, but he could feel it.

"Is that your 'thank you'?" Bee asked. "I'll take it."

"Thanks." Jessie leaned over his shallow bowl, inspecting the contents. He caught sight of red crawfish and half a seasoned corn cob sitting atop a bed of roasted potatoes. Everything was steaming-hot and smelled so fucking good. "You were gone a while."

"Did you miss me?" Bee picked up a crawfish as easily as if it had been stone cold. "It's fresh, don't complain." He cracked it apart and sucked the meat out in one draw, tossing the empty shell into the bucket when he was done.

"Just started wondering if you were ever going to come back." Jessie picked up a crawfish and pulled on the tail. Once the meat was free, he dragged it through a little plastic cup of melted butter that was wedged into the center of his bowl. "This place isn't so bad."

"I'm glad you approve." Bee reached over and handed Jessie a dark glass bottle. Jessie looked at it, then looked up at Bee, then looked back at the bottle. It didn't have a label.

"What is that?" Jessie asked.

"Root beer," Bee said.

Jessie didn't believe it, for some reason, but he took the bottle anyway and drank. It tasted like root beer that had clearly been mixed with something else. He couldn't tell if it was whiskey or rum. Jessie made a face and swiped his hand across his mouth, pausing to consider the bottle before taking another swig.

"Shit," he said after his second swallow. "That shit burns."

"I'd have thought you'd be impervious to it by now." Bee winked at him and drank from his own bottle. His bottle was clear, and the liquid inside was as blue as state fair cotton candy.

Jessie shot him a glare but drank again. He tasted less and less of the alcohol the more he drank. The bottle didn't seem to be getting any lower. It was always at least halfway full. The food had done its work to try and sober him up, but now his head was back to spinning. He took another bite and leaned back in his rocker, chasing the food down with several healthy swallows of his drink.

They sat there for a while and did not say much. It was hard for Jessie to take his eyes off Bee. There had always been something about the devil that just kept drawing his attention. As much as he hated himself for it, the whole reason he had stopped that day at the crossroads was because he couldn't resist the temptation of such a classically handsome face or the way Bee's broad shoulders pulled at his suit jacket whenever he moved. Up close, now, Bee's chest had just the right amount of sweat to make it glossy. His gold cross necklace was nestled against his dark, curling chest hair—and every now and then he would pick it up to stroke his fingers absentmindedly over the sharp corners. Behind his lavender glasses, his eyes seemed shuttered. His expression was distant, but nothing stopped him from pulling apart crawfish, sucking on them, and then tossing the shells. If there was anything on his mind, he was keeping it well to himself.

Pull. Suck. Toss.

Jessie swallowed. He turned his bottle around in his fingers and watched, fascinated by the vicious work of Bee's tongue and teeth moving in tandem. His strong fingers crumpled the shells like paper. He never looked where he threw them, but he made the shot every time.

Bee finally turned his head towards Jessie, and Jessie looked away. Moving his head so suddenly made the whole world swim. He gripped the arm of the rocking chair, feeling like he might fall out of it even though he hadn't moved anything else.

Jessie felt a hand touch his arm and slide up to his shoulder. Bee was humming something to himself, and it was at the exact decibel low enough to where Jessie couldn't figure out what it was supposed to be.

"What are you singing?" Jessie looked back at Bee, moving slowly this time. The devil was looking at him straight-on, and his gold tooth flashed in the porch light.

"*Look away, look away…*" his humming changed into soft crooning. He reached up a bit further and rested his finger against the soft underside of Jessie's chin. "*Look away…*" His drawl had gotten even thicker since they stepped off the plane. His voice was a bit deeper, no longer a fast-talking Texan but a gentle, easy Louisianan. He taunted Jessie with his mouth, getting close enough to flick his tongue over Jessie's bottom lip while his fingers pushed harder against the underside of his chin. A needy shiver racked Jessie's entire body. He felt Bee's hand on his thigh, scorching hot almost, and felt it travel up to slide through the leg of his boxers. A soft groan escaped his lips and Jessie tried to lower his head, but Bee kept him pinned in place. With the resistance, Bee pushed up a little more, making it so that Jessie had to lean his head back or choke. The devil's other hand continued its path until they found Jessie's warm, wet entrance.

"Slick," Bee whispered against his lips. "Already?" He stroked the outside, collecting the thick excretion on his fingers and sliding them up to swirl over Jessie's clit. "All I had to do was feed you."

Jessie wanted to say something, but all his words died in his throat. He whimpered impatiently, moving closer to the side of his chair so that Bee could get his hand further up. Bee pushed his fingers inside, using only two. He pushed them in up to the second knuckle and spread them apart. Jessie felt his insides stretch and he moaned again, squirming in his seat as he tried to push himself down. Bee did not give him a single inch more out of pity. He kept spreading his fingers and then pulling them out, stroking Jessie's clit and then pushing them back in. Jessie's breath came out in short, hot pants as felt his body tighten. When Bee had a mind, he knew how to push every single one of Jessie's buttons. Jessie slipped his hand under his own shirt and placed his hand against his chest, flicking his own nipple and squeezing a handful of his own chest. Bee purred at his desperation and slid his fingers in all the way up, grinding them against Jessie's cunt before teasing a third.

The intrusion of the third finger was enough to make Jessie writhe. He abandoned his chest and grabbed hold of the chair's arm, dragging his nails over the wood until he felt splinters jab at his fingers. Bee thrusted inside of him, pushing his fingers in as far as they would go, before twisting them around and pulling them back out. He stroked Jessie's clit again, slowly building up the pressure while moving his fingers in quick, tight circles. Jessie couldn't breathe. He was dizzy. His whole world was hot and humid and higher than the belly of a cloud. It sounded like cicadas and chirping bullfrogs. It tasted like corn liquor and root beer. He spread his legs and leaned back in his seat as his insides got tighter and tighter until the tension was like a steel string. His head hurt again, only because his brow was so scrunched up and he was clenching his teeth. He wanted to ask Bee to go down, but his tongue was frozen—wedged between his front teeth and in danger of being snicked off.

"Fuck!" Finally, a word, and it wasn't the one he wanted. Jessie banged his heel against a rocker and the pain that shot up his leg was enough to make him sit up. Bee grabbed his shoulder and pushed him back down. The sheer force of the devil's strength caused the headrest to bang against the wall. He held Jessie there, pinned against the rocking chair, pinned against the wall—and put his whole hand into rubbing Jessie's clit, while every now and then thrusting his fingers back inside.

Quick. Hot. Heavy. Wet. Jessie's orgasm shattered him. He threw his head forward and the sound that came out of his mouth was ragged and animalistic. He did not even recognize it as his own voice. He huffed out another breath, his whole body trembling as the pleasure swept over him in waves—like ripples through a puddle, they just kept rolling and swelling too rapidly to count.

Bee pulled out his hand right as Jessie was still deciding whether he wanted him to. The rocking chair swung forward as Bee loosened his hold and let Jessie up from the wall. Jessie sat there for a moment, unable to think at all. He was lost in the ecstasy of his post-orgasm rush and mourning the loss of Bee's hands at the same time. He allowed himself some time to just simmer in the moment. The darkness, the heat, the sluggish breeze.

Something wet prodded his hand. Jessie looked over, dazed, and saw that Bee was offering him a fresh bottle. This one had a label. Jessie took it gratefully.

"Just root beer," Bee said. "Cross my heart. You've had enough whiskey."

Jessie nodded his agreement and twisted off the top. The sharp metal hurt his hand, which was still sore from where he had been gripping the arm of his chair.

"I should go to bed," Jessie said. He hoped his words sounded a little clearer to Bee than they did to his own ears.

"Yes." Bee drummed his glistening fingers against the arm of his own rocker. "You should."

CHAPTER THREE

THE SWEET PRICE OF AN EVERLASTING SOUL

The next day it rained. Jessie's head felt like it had been stuffed full of oatmeal and the pressure from the storm only made it worse. Rain spattered against the windows from behind gauzy curtains, pouring down from a sky so dark that it might as well have been night. Jessie rolled back onto his side and pulled the thin cover up over his head, content to go back to sleep if he could manage it.

The overhead light flicked on. He growled and pushed his face into the pillow.

"You are acting like someone who doesn't want breakfast," Bee said.

"I don't," Jessie said. "I want to go back to sleep."

"You've slept plenty," Bee told him. "Do you know what time it is?"

"No." Jessie dug his toes against the mattress, as if that could anchor him to the bed.

"It's almost ten," Bee said. "Get up and get dressed."

"It's *pouring*." Jessie's head hurt too much to keep arguing. "My head fucking hurts."

Bee slammed a glass down on the bedside table. The contents looked slimy and dark with bites of white floating around—and it smelled like Worcestershire sauce. Jessie's stomach churned.

"I don't think so," Jessie muttered.

"Jessie." Bee's tone was shorter than Jessie was used to. "Don't make me drag you out of bed."

Jessie shouldn't have been confused about Bee's sudden shift in mood from the night before, but he was. He didn't remember much past getting in bed—in fact, he was pretty sure he had fallen asleep almost immediately. Not a lot could have occurred between Jessie getting fingered—which Bee seemed to enjoy plenty—and him falling asleep that could have ticked the devil off. It didn't matter, really, because Jessie still didn't feel like dealing with it. He sat up and grabbed the glass. The contents looked even worse from above, but if he didn't drink it, Bee might try pouring it down his throat. He pinched his nose and drank it down like medicine. Afterward, all he could taste was vinegar and salt. Jessie gagged and covered his mouth with the back of his hand, trying his best not to let nausea win.

"Good boy," the devil said. Bee walked around the side of the bed and shoved his fingers through Jessie's sweaty curls. "I laid out something for you to wear."

"I can dress myself," Jessie argued.

"You sure?" Bee scoffed. "You're moving too slow for me. I'm going to have breakfast. If you want anything to eat, then you can meet me there."

"Where are you going?" Jessie asked. He looked over at the clothes Bee had set out for him—what looked like a pair of long black pants and a loose black tank.

"I don't intend to linger," Bee went on without answering his question. "So don't keep me waiting." His words were laced with warning. Jessie didn't respond and Bee left without giving any more information and without closing the bedroom door.

Jessie was tempted to go back to sleep, but he knew that it wasn't what he was *supposed* to do. Bee wanted to be followed. He wanted Jessie to look for him. If Jessie didn't try, there would be consequences—and not the fun kind, either. More likely the kind that left him feeling numb with a mouthful of blood.

Jessie dressed himself quickly and made his way towards the front door. His regular shoes, that Bee hated, were waiting by the sink where he had taken them off before the whole casino adventure. He slipped them on and made sure he had his wallet before he left. He didn't have a key, so he made sure the door clicked when he shut it and hoped that no one had a mind to break in.

There was a bright blue umbrella left propped up by the door. Jessie picked it up and pushed the button on the handle to release it. Rain streamed off the front porch's gutter-less roof and splattered on the concrete steps in hard, fast drops. It sounded like someone pissing.

Jessie's shoes were immediately soaked as soon as he stepped off the porch, which was almost enough to make him have a meltdown, but he kept going. He had no idea where Bee was, and the best way to find him was to just head towards the main street and start looking. Worst case scenario, he got some breakfast out of it but still didn't find Bee. He didn't know what the consequences would be for trying and still not winning the game, but that was something he intended to worry about after he'd had some coffee.

The first three restaurants he stuck his head into had no sign of Bee. He tried everywhere that looked like it might appeal to the devil—a corner café, a European-style pub, and a coffee house that bragged in every window about its homemade donuts. The food smells in each place, combined with all the walking, were starting to get to him. The rain, too—the streets were full of water and his shoes slogged through every puddle. He stopped at the very next door with a neon '*OPEN*' sign and let himself in, resolved to get himself some food with or without his hellish partner.

The diner he chose was nearly empty. Jessie didn't mind that at all and shook the water off his umbrella before going to seat himself at the counter. The waiter, a scraggly blonde who looked like he hadn't slept in eight years, didn't even turn around. Jessie drummed his fingers against the counter and waited, looking around to try and soak everything in. There was nothing special about it. Same black and white linoleum on the floor as anywhere else, same salmon-pink laminate countertops, same cushioned stools that made sounds like a trumpeting fart when he sat down...

"How can I help you?"

Jessie jerked and turned his attention to the blonde waiter. Up close, he was cute, but in the vague sense that Jessie thought anyone with sideburns and glasses was cute. His nametag said that his name was Leslie.

"Uhh," Jessie rubbed his face. "Do you have coffee?"

"Sure do," Leslie said. "Decaf or regular?"

Jessie wanted to know if he *actually* looked like someone who went anywhere to drink decaf. "Regular. Please. With cream and sugar."

"All right. Do you want anything to eat?"

"Sure." Jessie spread his hands. "Do you have a menu?"

Leslie made a face that said he was being dreadfully inconvenienced and reached across the counter to the empty spot next to Jessie. He slammed his hand down on a glossy, faded menu and slid it over without even trying to pick it up.

"Thanks," Jessie muttered. "I'll just need a minute."

"Take your time," Leslie said. "I'll get that coffee going." He walked away, a little less attractive because Jessie despised people with snotty attitudes.

"I recommend the Belgian waffles," a voice that Jessie did not recognize entered the mix. "You can get them with strawberries or chocolate."

Jessie gripped his menu a little too tightly and looked around for the source. "I don't really like strawberries," he said. "They're gritty."

The person who spoke was standing far too close. They had inserted themselves between Jessie and the next barstool over and still had plenty of room to take a step back. Jessie tried not to look as upset as he felt. One stranger interaction at a time was pretty much all he was equipped to handle, and Leslie was the one who could bring him coffee.

"Then I would definitely get them with chocolate," the stranger said. "Believe me when I say they're out of this world and they came on a plate as big as your head."

"Sounds great." If compliance earned him some peace, Jessie was willing to try anything. The stranger didn't seem put off at all by his short responses.

"My name is Abel," they said. They took a step back, but it was only to slide onto the barstool next to Jessie. He groaned inwardly.

"I'm Jessie," he said. Now that they were further back, he took a better look. They were dressed for the weather in a soft gray peacoat that was unbuttoned, and underneath they were wearing a dark blue V-neck that plunged down past their sun-kissed collarbone. Their soft, mink-brown hair was long enough to curl around their ears while their brown eyes, only a slightly darker shade, had flecks of orange and green like freshly-turned autumn leaves. A pair of rectangular tortoise-shell glasses sat on the bridge of their hawkish nose, and at that point Jessie had to look away. They seemed to notice he was staring.

"I don't think we've met before," Abel said. "I would have remembered." They had a pretty nice smile. Jessie looked back down at the menu and picked at his short nails.

"I'm not that memorable," he said. "But this is my first time here."

"Your first time?" Their eyes sparkled. "That's magical. I wish I could be in your shoes, walking down Bourbon Street at night for the very first—"

"Here's your coffee." Brown liquid sloshed over the sides of the short white mug as Leslie-the-waiter set it down. The spilled coffee made a little ring on the counter, but he did not make any efforts to wipe it up. He pulled out his thinning paper pad and clicked the end of his pen against it pointedly. "Are you ready to order?"

"Yeah." Jessie was relieved to have an excuse to abandon the conversation. "I'll have a waffle, please, with eggs— over easy—and bacon."

"Anything on the waffle?"

"Just butter." Jessie placed his menu back down.

Leslie ripped the piece of paper off his pad and turned away from the counter. He didn't address Abel at all, which Jessie thought was weird, but he also didn't blame him.

Abel did not seem bothered in the least. They hadn't even turned away—which Jessie had hoped they would.

"How long are you going to be in the city?" Abel asked.

Jessie shrugged. "Dunno," he said. "Until my boyfriend decides it's time to go home." It was weird to refer to Bee as his 'boyfriend', even for the sake of simplicity.

"I see," Abel said. They didn't bat their eye at the mention of a boyfriend. "Where is home?"

"Texas," Jessie muttered.

"Where in Texas?"

"Why do you want to know so badly?" Jessie pushed his blunt thumbnails into the sides of his fingers, trying to stay calm and keep his voice level.

"Just curiosity," Abel admitted. "I like the way you talk, and I want to hear you do it more."

Jessie would have preferred being told that Abel was scoping him out for a murder. He pinched up two packets of sugar from a nearby tray and started shaking them.

"What about you, then?" He figured that he might as well ask, since he was stuck until his breakfast arrived. "Where do you come from?"

Abel went quiet. They took so long to answer that Jessie's waffle arrived and he ended up looking over to see whether or not they had left.

No, Abel was still sitting on their stool, their brown eyes staring right through Jessie.

"Roanoke," they finally said, perking back up as if letting out an answer rejuvenated them. "Virgnia. No place like it in the world."

"Bet not." Jessie turned his attention towards eating. Roanoke was eerily close to Richmond, where he had been born, but he did not want to bring that up.

"Say," Abel continued, "you are not going to try and walk back all by yourself, are you? Let me go with you."

"I can manage," Jessie said, hooking one foot over the rung underneath his stool. "I need to learn the city anyway."

"Today is not the day for that. It is still pouring." Abel ducked their head to look out the window as if double-checking to make sure they were not, in fact, a liar.

"I will be fine." Jessie finished his waffle in fewer bites than he should have and dashed it down with the bitter diner coffee. Leaving as quickly as possible was suddenly a way more appealing option than letting his food settle, and there was no telling when the rain would stop. "Bee…" he stopped himself there.

"Oh, I see." Abel tilted their head. "Is your boyfriend the jealous type?"

"Only in the sense that he is food aggressive." Out of context, Jessie realized that the comparison made no sense to anyone but himself. He waved his hand, dismissing it. "I have to go." He reached for his wallet, belatedly scrambling to remember which cards were in there, if any of them were Bee's and if the ones that were his had enough of a balance to pay ten dollars plus tip.

"It is on me," Abel said as they stood. Jessie's eyes followed them, and he picked up his coffee to take one more sip.

"Thanks," he said. "I—thanks."

"Don't mention it." Abel picked up a bright yellow umbrella that Jessie hadn't seen before and swung it up to rest against their shoulder. "Be safe out there, Jessie Livingston."

They left, then, opening up their big yellow umbrella as soon as they were out the door. Jessie watched them leave. There was a tightness in his stomach like someone had wrapped their fist around it and started squeezing.

He had never mentioned his last name.

Jessie looked back at his plate. Of course, the chatty stranger had been too forgetful to pay. He waved down the waiter.

"Can I get the ticket?" he asked as he fished again for his wallet.

Leslie blinked at him, looking more confused than anything.

"You already paid just a minute ago," he said. "Do you want something else?"

Jessie didn't like that. He didn't know much about the supernatural, but he had spent enough time with Bee to know he didn't want to fuck around with it more than he already had. He shivered and rubbed at the goosebumps that appeared on his arm.

"No," he said. "Sorry. Thanks." He slid off the stool and grabbed his umbrella, only to notice that his hands were shaking.

If he had not intended to go back to the cottage before, he was now. Bee was bound to circle back eventually whether or not he caught up. Screw it.

Jessie gripped his umbrella tight and checked to make sure there were no lingering signs of Abel before bolting out.

Darkness slithered around on the rain-slick cottage porch. Its thick tendrils squeezed through every opening, curling around the railing balusters and creeping down the shallow front steps that ended in a cracked cement path. It was invisible to anyone who didn't know what they were looking at, especially through the rain, but it told Jessie two things; it told him that Bee was inside, and that he was probably pissed.

Bee's bad moods, like everything else about him, were infectious. They had habit of oozing out like molasses and getting stuck on everything they touched. Jessie skirted the porch to try and avoid it, walking around the side of the cottage instead to try and poke around for a window. If the front door had Bee's mood all over it, then the back was probably just as bad. He resolved to try it anyway if his window plan fell through.

The rain was still coming down, hard, and his shoes sank into the mud. The bedroom window had a soft, rotted sill where there was enough of a gap underneath the pane that he could potentially slip something through. Jessie tucked the umbrella handle underneath his armpit and fished in his pockets for his knife. The blade was small, but the tip curved into a sharp point. He jammed it underneath and wiggled it back and forth a few times, turning it over onto its side and chipping away at the wood. He cleared some more of it away and then stuck his fingers underneath. It wasn't locked very well at the top. The dark metal piece was the kind that turned with a little knob and it was hanging most of the way out of place. Considering there was no screen he could only assume that it hadn't been used in a while. Jessie set his teeth and pushed up as hard as he could, gripping the bottom tightly so that his hand did not slip. The frame groaned and he kept pushing. He allowed the umbrella to fall in order to give himself more leverage and kicked it aside so that he could step closer. The lock at the top eventually popped and his hand shot up as the window slid on its track. It didn't stop until it banged against the top rail and he winced, but he did not waste any time before crawling through. He decided he would come back for the umbrella later.

Jessie's hands hit the floor and he dragged the rest of his body through. He dragged his knees up to his chest and stayed hunkered against the ground for a minute longer than he meant to, pushing out a series of ragged breaths while shivering miserably on the dark wood. He listened for any signs of Bee's whereabouts, but he could not really hear much outside of his own heartbeat and the thunder that rattled the cottage.

"What kept you?" Bee's voice came out of nowhere like a crack of lightning and he slammed the window back down into place. Jessie flinched at the sudden noise and tried to push himself up.

"I couldn't find you," Jessie said. Even as he spoke, he felt Bee's shoe slam into his back, and the devil ground his heel between Jessie's shoulders as he pushed him back down to the ground.

"Piss-poor excuse for not doing as you are told," Bee said. "And then you come back here looking like something the alligator dragged in."

Jessie bit his cheek until it bled. The faint, coppery taste and the sting was the only thing that grounded him. "I was trying to avoid your pissy little mood."

"Well, you failed." Bee pushed down a little harder until Jessie could no longer breathe easily. "You are the reason for my '*pissy little mood*'. What did you find while you were out? I hope it was worth it."

"Nothing," Jessie snapped. "A diner. Let me up!"

"A diner?" Bee didn't sound like he believed it. "You stink of brimstone."

"What?" Jessie's arms started to shake with exertion. "I don't know what—"

"Did you meet anyone?" Bee removed his foot. Jessie shot up to his knees as quickly as he could and then stood, using the wall as a support.

"One person." There was no use in lying. Jessie sniffed and dragged his hand across his nose. "They wouldn't leave me alone. I guess two if you count the waiter." He tacked on the last bit just to be smart.

"So, you avoided me—" Bee began.

"I wasn't avoiding you!"

"—You *avoided me,*" Bee continued, widening his eyes behind his lavender glasses and clenching his teeth as he spoke. "You dallied with some hell-born hussy and then you come crawling back—through the window, even, like a criminal—smelling like sulfur. It's almost like you've got a clue about how much shit you're in."

Jessie shook his head. "You are blowing this way out of proportion," he said. "You left and I followed. I did *as I was told.*"

"*No,*" Bee snarled. "If you had done as you were *told,* then you would have been up and ready to leap when I said jump." He moved closer, circling Jessie like a fox scoping out a hen. "So, what was their name?"

"I don't remember." Jessie searched his spinning thoughts. "Abel, I think. You know, the famous Grand Duke of He—" his words were cut off when Bee grabbed his jaw. The devil squeezed hard enough that it felt like the bone was going to crack. Jessie winced in pain and grabbed Bee's wrist in response, but the devil's grip was iron, and he was too strong. Jessie couldn't pull away from him.

"Don't get smart with me," Bee warned. Another clap of thunder shook the entire cottage. Bee kept one hand on Jessie while the other reached up to pull his round sunglasses away from his face. Jessie tried to look away, but Bee twisted his head around until their eyes were forced to meet. Those damning blue eyes—the same vivid shade as Texas bluebonnets in the spring. They lingered long enough that Jessie could feel the tips of his fingers start to tingle.

"No." It was hard for Jessie to speak with Bee's splayed fingers pressing into his cheeks, but he decided to make one last-ditch effort to defend himself. "No, Bee, I'm sorry…please…"

The tingling began to spread. He could feel it his toes, now, and a spasm shot down his leg—making it jerk. He almost lost his balance, but Bee kept him upright.

"It seems like such a small thing," Bee cooed, although his softening voice held its razor edge. "I never ask you to do much of anything, really. The terms of our deal are very lax. In fact, I like to think of us as more than just devil-and-consort. We are good friends, aren't we, Jessie-beau?"

The old term of endearment slipped off his tongue as if it did not have the power to bring Jessie to his knees. Bee only liked to dust it off for special occasions, like when he really wanted something. If Jessie had not already been grappling with the creeping, cold numbness taking over his body, it would have been enough to melt him into submission.

Jessie tried to talk again, but his tongue felt thick and too big for his mouth. His mouth was filling up and he could not swallow, no matter how hard he tried. He put all his focus on keeping his breath circulating through his nose, while Bee's ink-black pupils kept getting bigger and bigger, almost swallowing his blue-bonnet irises. Jessie mouth slackened, and he knew that he was drooling, although he couldn't feel it. He couldn't feel anything anymore. Bee's eyes became his entire world, drawing him in and rolling him under.

Rolling. That was what Bee called it.

Through the numbness, there was suddenly pain. It shot through Jessie's intestines and made his stomach turn. He groaned and he tried to turn his head again, but Bee kept him locked in place.

"Did you eat?" Bee's words were barely audible, but his voice dragged along the inside of Jessie's skull like iron nails. "Are you very, very full?"

Jessie's stomach flipped again. A wave of nausea seized him, and his body convulsed as vomit shot up his throat. He could feel it, a little bit, coming through his nose and he could taste the bitter stomach acid mixed with everything he had eaten that morning. Bee let him go, and Jessie was vaguely aware of falling. He heard—rather than felt—his head crack against the floor and bounce. Once the eye contact was broken, the pain caught up to him like an ice pick being driven into the back of his skull. Any sound he might have made was smothered in his own vomit, but the feeling hadn't returned back to his limbs, so he was stuck on his back.

Bee stood over him, legs spread over Jessie's hips as he slipped his lavender glasses back on. His shirt was covered in vomit, which it did not have to be. He wanted it there. He wanted Jessie's shame and guilt.

"Look at you," he said. He nudged the side of his shoe against Jessie's ribs. "Pathetic. Helpless. Choking on your own vomit." He just stood there, watching. "I should let you."

Jessie gagged and more vomit came up. His mouth and nose burned while his whole body fought for survival. The numbness wasn't fading fast enough, but like a bad dream he kept trying to move his arms and legs—*anything* to help him turn over faster.

He had enough time to think about what it would be like for the person who found him. Bee certainly wasn't going to stick around with a corpse. He wondered what his corpse would look like. Maybe purple from lack of air, covered in ugly yellow spew.

Bee stepped over him and nudged his ribs once again. This time, the devil applied enough pressure to roll Jessie over onto his side. Jessie coughed up as much vomit as he could, emptying everything that had pooled in his mouth and then more. By the time it was done, his nose and chest hurt too much to take a breath.

Jessie dragged his hand across his nose and then his sleeve, not caring how much Bee hated it.

"That is absolutely disgusting, Jessie-beau," Bee said after a moment. "You are going to have to get it all cleaned up."

CHAPTER FOUR

AN OUNCE OF FLESH

The spinning white ball on the roulette wheel was the only thing that could hold Jessie's attention. Everything else around him was a blur of sound and light. His stomach still hurt, but Bee had dragged him out of bed anyway to get to the casino. After their last discussion, he was not eager to upset the devil again.

Bee didn't appear too invested in the game itself. From the way the dealer's hands kept trembling and jerking, he was far more interested in what trouble he could cause. Jessie recognized the look that kept creeping up onto the man's face. Bee was doing what he did best—he was digging at the back of the poor guy's brain and unearthing every lurid thought and desire, twisting it around and turning it into something inescapable. Twitching hands was just one sign. The dealer's eyes kept flitting back and forth, as if there was a possibility someone might overhear whatever was bouncing around the inside of his skull. That was another. He kept licking his lips, which was probably just a nervous tic that Bee was making worse just by sitting there. Jessie knew what that was like. He dragged his hand across his nose.

"Hit me," Bee winked. If he caught the dealer's eyes, it would all be over. Like a fish on a line, it would only take a single hook. Watching the guy struggle against such a violent, unnatural force was sort of pitiful. Jessie hoped he was the only one who noticed. Otherwise, it would just be sick voyeurism.

Jessie rubbed his nose again. This time, his fingers came back bloody, leading into a trail of dark red slime that cut a wide path over his knuckles and ended at his wrist.

"Shit!" Jessie covered nose with his bloody hand, pinching his nostrils to try and stop the flow. He stole a glance at Bee, but the devil's back was turned, and the last thing Jessie wanted to do was interrupt the hunt playing out in front of him.

He knew that he should. Grabbing Bee's nice suit jacket with a bloody hand and breaking his focus would be enough to potentially save a man's life—or at least his sanity, which seemed to be slipping away a little faster with each passing second. However, the dealer wasn't Jessie's problem.

Jessie abandoned them both and headed for the bar. He tried not to gag on the blood running down the back of his throat and failed, coughing into his hand until it spurted from between his fingers. A few people who had been standing in his way suddenly gave him a wide berth. The bartender looked him up and down, giving him enough consideration to curl his lip in disgust before walking away.

Jessie swerved, trying to spot a bathroom. He didn't *want* to spew blood all over the counter, but he would, if that was what it took to get a towel.

One of the nearby patrons turned in their seat and plucked up the bartender's discarded rag. It was a little damp from the looks of it, but they held it up anyway and offered it to Jessie.

"Here you are." The dingy rag dangled from the tips of their gloved fingers. "You look a sight."

Jessie recognized the voice. He snatched the damp rag and pressed it against his nose to stop the bleeding. It smelled a little bit like cleaning chemicals, which was probably a bad thing, but he didn't care at that moment.

"I remember you," Jessie said, his voice slightly muffed by the terrycloth. "You got me into some deep shit."

Abel grabbed the rim of their glasses' frame and adjusted them on their nose, looking offended.

"Did I?" they asked. "Well, then I apologize."

Jessie leaned against the bar and glared at the polished, pitted surface. "You could have mentioned that you were a devil. Would have saved us both a lot of time."

Abel laughed, a mixture of sharp astonishment and faint delight. "A devil? Well, all right. Why not?"

Jessie ground his teeth. "Don't laugh at me." He pulled the cloth away to check for more blood. "Like I said, I was in deep shit because of you."

"Is that why your nose is bleeding?" Abel tilted their head.

"No," Jessie said. "I think I just got lucky." The bleeding finally stopped. He set the soiled rag back down on the counter, resisting the urge to toss into an ice bucket for the snippy bartender to find later.

"You seem to have a lot of luck, if that's the case." Abel pushed their glass across the counter. "Have a sip. You look like you need it."

Jessie picked up the glass and swished around the brown alcohol inside doubtfully. "I should get back." He glanced over his shoulder. He couldn't see Bee through the crowd, which only made him more nervous.

"What were you playing?" Abel asked. The bartender came back over to ruefully sweep up the bloody rag and Abel held up two fingers. "Two more bourbons, please," they said, "neat."

Jessie knocked back what was left in the glass he had been given. "Blackjack," he said.

"I prefer poker." Abel smiled. They wore their gray suit jacket draped over their shoulders and what looked like a pinstripe vest underneath at first glance, but the ridges of boning bowing underneath the fabric gave it away as a corset. Their gloves were supple yellow leather and made their already-slender fingers look even slimmer. Jessie could see them being a poker fiend. He wasn't sure why— it was just the way they carried themselves.

"Bee doesn't really like poker," Jessie said, glancing over his shoulder again just to be sure that Bee had not suddenly materialized behind him.

"It requires a great deal of strategy," Abel said demurely, "perhaps that is why."

Jessie choked. He set his empty glass down and picked up the fresh drink brought over by the bartender. "It's not that he's impatient," he said. "He's actually the most patient person I know. He will lie in wait for an opportunity—you know, like a crocodile."

"I did not call him impatient," Abel said, "I implied he doesn't like to think ahead."

The bourbon made Jessie's tongue warm. He swished it around his mouth, swiping his tongue over his cheeks for any lingering notes of flavor. His nose still burned a little, but for the most part he felt all right. He knew he should get back. It was hard to convince himself to move.

Abel's brown-sugar gaze lingered over him for a long minute before they pulled out a gold cigarette case. "I am going to have a smoke." They gestured towards the door. "Why don't you step outside with me?"

"I should get back," Jessie said.

"To what?" Abel stood. "Besides, you look like you could use some air."

It was hot outside, but it was stuffy inside the casino. It was loud, too. The idea of stepping away from the flashing lights and constant stream of noises was more tempting an offer than a change in air.

Jessie gave it another second of consideration before he followed Abel out. He tucked his hands into his slack pockets so he could curl his fingers up in the satin lining and drive his blunt nails against his thigh. Crossing the threshold without Bee did not feel liberating as he thought it might. If anything, it made his chest feel constricted, and he paused to pull in a struggling breath.

Abel looked over at him with what read as vague concern, although nothing stopped them from tugging a cigarette free from its case and sticking it onto the end of a long black cigarette holder. They placed the bitten end between their teeth and smoke soon streamed out from the separation of their soft, pillowy lips. "So," they said. "Tell me how you ended up like this."

"Like what?" Jessie hugged his own chest.

Abel pulled the cigarette holder from their lips and gestured vaguely. "You don't seem like much of a gambling man," they said. "And every time I've run into you it's been like extending my hand to a shelter dog. You know me for a devil and that is not something most people can sus out on their own. So, I want to know—how does a little bumpkin like you end up in a city like this?"

Jessie resented the word 'bumpkin', but he had been called worse. He thought about lying, but something about

Abel made him feel compelled to tell the truth. It was almost like the words came bubbling up his throat like foam, too frothy and loose to swallow. He dragged his nose over his knuckles and huffed against his own skin.

"I was coming out of church," he finally said. "I don't usually go. I was there because I..." he took a deep breath. "Well, I set a couple of razors on the bathroom counter that morning and I figured I might as well give myself one last shot at repentance. I thought maybe the sermon would make me feel something, like maybe there would be a parable about a lost sheep returning to the fold or some shit that would give me second thoughts. The pastor ended up going on a rant about the end times and the sins of homosexuality which—I should have expected. And for me, you know, I had already lost everything. I lost my apartment in Dallas, my job, and my girlfriend. I was at the point where I pretty much figured that no one would ever take me seriously as a man. So, ending everything and hoping for a better reincarnation seemed like a logical step."

Abel nodded and took another drag from their cigarette. "You got an offer you were not expecting from a hand you could not refuse?"

"Something like that." Jessie rubbed the back of his neck. "I met Bee standing at the crossroads and he was just so— damn irresistible. It was like stopping at a crosswalk and looking down to see a hundred-dollar bill. He was just so shiny and—*slick.* Prettier than a new car, and he just—I don't know, you probably know—everything that came out of his mouth just made so much sense."

Abel exhaled another cloud. "He offered to make you a man?"

"Yeah. It's been gradual. More body hair, deeper voice— flatter chest."

Abel smiled. "A cock?"

Jessie rolled his eyes. "I didn't ask for one."

"Fair enough." Abel looked as though they were mulling over their next thought. Their silence lasted long enough that Jessie became aware of his own sticky forehead and the gnats swarming his ankles.

"What do you like about him, then?" Abel asked.

"What do you mean?" Jessie swatted at a gnat.

"Devils, demons, they don't stick around where they aren't wanted." Abel shrugged. "They have better things to do than try and squeeze blood out of a turnip. So, there's something about him that makes you *like* him."

Jessie hesitated. "I guess...I'm comfortable around him," he said. "I'm myself around him. And it's easy to forget sometimes that all I am to him is food. He's pushy, he's cruel, and he doesn't care about my feelings—he likes to push me past my boundaries, but at the end of the day, he lets me exist as I am. That's worth something for however long it lasts."

"It is worth something," Abel agreed. "You are the only one who can determine whether it's a fair price for what you are selling."

The answer sounded vague to Jessie, but he just shrugged it away. He was starting to get a bit of a buzz from the secondhand smoke and it made his anxiety ramp back up. Bee was looking for him. He could *feel* it.

If he was caught with Abel, he was as good as dead or worse. He didn't want to think about what Bee would do to him.

"I have to go." He turned back towards the front entrance. "It was nice...talking to you." The words faltered on his tongue, seeming insincere, but he was not sure what else to say. Thankfully, Abel did not try to wring anything more out of him.

"Ciao." The devil winked. "Enjoy yourself. I will see you again."

Jessie took that as a threat. He pulled the casino door open so fast that he nearly smacked himself in the face and darted through before Abel could say anything else.

Bee was still sitting at the blackjack table when Jessie returned. All the other seats around him were empty except the stool right next to him where he had draped his blazer. The dealer looked a little pale, even under the yellow light right above his head. He kept putting his hands to his mouth in-between doling out the cards like he was chewing on his nails, and the gnawing made a grisly sound that Jessie could hear even over the din.

Jessie grabbed an empty seat beside the devil and Bee looked over, touching the side of his sunglasses.

"Did you miss me?" Jessie asked, an empty echo of Bee's words.

"Maybe," Bee said. "Did you finally stop bleeding?"

"Eventually." Jessie flicked his eyes over at the dealer. "What is with him?" he whispered.

"Him?" Bee's smile spread across his mouth like an oil stain. "He skipped lunch."

Jessie furrowed his brow and glanced down at the blackjack table. All the cards had faint, rust-colored smears across their white faces. "What?"

"Hit me," Bee said. Another card came down to rest on top of the stack. The dealer's fingertips were dark red and looked crumpled, ground down like the chewed-up end of a pencil. He stuck them back in his mouth immediately after setting down the card, and Jessie caught a flash of his bloodstained teeth grinding down on his fingertip like a candy stick.

"Shit." Jessie held onto his stool and leaned forward, gripping it tight enough that his knuckles went white. "Bee, what the hell?" He kept his voice low even though he wasn't worried about the dealer overhearing him anymore. The man's entire world had been narrowed down to only two things—his hunger, and Bee's voice.

"I told you." Bee dashed his tongue across his gold canine. "I just did a little digging. Our friend here is hungry for a lot of things. He is *desperate,* I would say, for something to go right. He didn't eat lunch because there was nothing in his fridge to pack this morning. He has already spent twelve hours on his feet and he has no one to go home to. Can't you feel it?"

"No," Jessie said. "You know I can't."

Bee picked up the card resting on top of the stack and flipped it around. "He is starving. He wants companionship, he wants money—he wants it all so badly. The physical hunger, those deep pains in his stomach, were the easiest to grab hold of." He looked at Jessie. "He can't hang onto it forever. It must be satisfied. How desperate would you say he is? Let's make a bet."

"I don't want to," Jessie muttered. "I want to go back to our room. It's hot in here, and loud."

Bee waved the card around in front of Jessie's eyes, a hypnotic side-to-side motion like a quivering cobra. "Come on now, Jessie-beau. I would say he's hungry enough to chew his fingers to the bone, but he's already doing that. So, let's get more creative." He glanced around the room. "Hungry enough to go to the bar, drink a bottle down, and eat the glass. What do you think?"

"Is there any use betting against you?" Jessie asked, resigned. "What do I get if I win?"

"Then you can call the next bet."

"I see. What if you win?"

"If I win?" Bee flipped the card around again. "You give me anything I ask for."

Jessie took a deep breath. "All right." His words felt squeezed out of his chest. "All right. I don't think he will eat the glass."

"That is the spirit." The card was turning black underneath Bee's fingertips. When he rotated it again, it was just like one that had been pulled from his own deck—completely black with only a little sporadic spot-shine to indicate the numbers and suits. He turned it again and brought it to rest face-down on the table, smacking the corner against the green speed cloth.

At the crisp, sudden sound, the dealer looked up. There was something harrowing in his eyes—a deep, unsettling darkness like staring down into an unlit cellar. The hunger lived there. It scratched at the sides of his pupils, twin pinpricks of white light that that circled the vacuous black holes like fingers clawing to get out. He swiped his tongue over his bloody bottom lip, leaving a shiny wet path that he dragged down with his ruined fingertips. More blood smeared along his chin, but it was like he did not even notice. If he was in any pain, it did not register on his face.

To Jessie, he looked like he was already dead.

"Not playing fair," Jessie breathed, "if you've already got control of his mind."

"It's not control," Bee said. "I just gave the appetite a nudge."

The dealer pulled himself out from behind the table, swinging his head around until his empty eyes settled on the bar. Jessie and Bee stood up to follow him, since the bar was just out of their range of sight. The dealer stumbled over as if he could not quite keep control of his legs. His knees wobbled and he had to grasp onto the bar for support. Underneath the brighter neon lights, Jessie caught a glimpse of white bone when his chewed fingers gripped the counter.

There was already a half-empty beer bottle waiting to be swept up when he got there. The dealer grabbed it and put it to his lips, his hands trembling as he drank down the rest of the pale gold brew in three enormous swallows. The glass rim never left his mouth. He rotated it over the edge of his bottom teeth, turning it in his hand and staring across the counter, searching for more. He did not even seem to comprehend what he was doing as he set his top row of teeth against the bottle's grooves, pushing it all the way into his cheek until it rested against his back molars. There was a brief, horrible pause before Jessie heard the glass crack.

"Shit," Jessie said. "Bee, make him stop."

"A little late for that." Bee still had the black playing card in his hands. He flipped it around, weaving it through his fingers as he watched the scene play out. "He's already swallowed glass. It's over."

Jessie's nose suddenly itched something fierce. He rubbed his fingers irately against the tip. "What now?" The sound of glass being ground against human teeth made him want to throw up. "I have to give you anything you ask for, right?"

"Right," Bee said.

"Seems like a bad bet," Jessie said bitterly. "Don't you get that anyway?"

"I think you are missing the point," Bee said. "It isn't about what I could take, it's about what you can give me freely." He adjusted his sunglasses again. "I want an ounce of flesh."

"An ounce?" Jessie scoffed under his breath, even though his stomach clenched at the words. "Why not a pound?"

"Would you give it to me?" Bee grinned. "An ounce will do."

"All right." Jessie looked around. He skipped his gaze over the unfortunate card dealer, whose mouth was coated in blood. Jagged points of broken glass protruded from his tattered throat—not that anyone seemed to notice. The rest of the patrons moved through the casino as if nothing unusual was occurring. They seemed to simply *miss* the grisly sight. It was Bee's way. All the little flies stuck to his web became so easy to overlook.

"Do you want to go back, then?" Jessie asked. His eyes settled back on Bee. The devil turned to face him, and in that same second, his heart jumped into his throat. Maybe it was the heat that radiated off Bee's body, or maybe it was the way he looked at Jessie from behind lavender lenses like a panther sizing up his prey. Jessie's mouth went dry, and he rubbed his own arm for comfort, scraping his blunt nails over the scabby bumps on his skin.

"No," Bee said. "We can do it right here. I don't think anyone is going to notice." He winked. The way his upper lip curled exposed his gleaming gold canine. Jessie's knees almost gave out underneath him.

"Not if you don't want them to," Jessie said. "I don't want anyone to see me."

"What do you think I'm going to do to you, hm?" Bee tilted his head and cocked a dark eyebrow. "What do you take me for?" He closed the distance between them and slid his hands underneath Jessie's jacket, resting them against the bend of his waist. His skin was unbearably warm. Jessie could feel it radiating through his thin dress shirt.

"I take you for what you are," Jessie groaned, "a devil."

"And that is why we get along so well." Bee lifted Jessie up as if he weighed nothing at all and set him on a barstool. "I take you as you are, and you take me as I am. We do all right that way."

Jessie couldn't breathe. He grabbed hold of Bee's shoulders, closing his eyes against the increasing sounds of grinding glass and wet gurgling—and over that, in the distance, triumphant shouts and singing slot machines. "Bee…"

"Relax," Bee purred. He leaned in close enough that his lips brushed over the shell of Jessie's ear, and he dragged his fingertips down the line of his trembling jaw. "Unclench."

Jessie's teeth ached, but he could not relax his jaw. He could feel every wet, heavy thud from his heart behind his ribs. Each beat made his jugular throb and sent pain all the way up to his temple. The pain pooled behind his eye and made it water, while every breath felt stifled from the heat. He placed his hands against Bee's chest, for what little good it did him. He could not fend off the devil, even if he wanted to.

The rub of it all was that for all the pain, he *wanted* Bee to come closer. He wanted Bee's tongue, his mouth, his teeth. He wanted his iron fingers and his sharp nails. He wanted to be consumed. He wanted, he wanted, he *wanted…*

'Tell me how you ended up like this.' Abel's voice echoed in his head. There really wasn't a question.

Bee's hands slid over his shoulders and down the front of his chest. For a quick second, panic brought Jessie's head up, and he watched Bee sink down to one knee in front of him. Once again, no one seemed to notice. There were people all around them. The bartender sprayed seltzer from a nozzle. A couple argued nearby, but their words sounded like useless babble.

Slot machines screamed. Neon and fluorescent lights buzzed.

"It is so bright in here." Jessie swiped his sleeve across his brow. His cuff came back soaked with sweat.

"Keep your eyes one me." Bee's wicked hands trailed down Jessie's calf, sliding over every curve through his straight black slacks. He cupped the heel of Jessie's white leather wing-tip oxford at the end and raised it to rest against his own knee. The devil worked at the laces, unknotting them without much effort, and slid the shoe away. Self-conscious revulsion that Jessie could not explain crawled up the back of his neck as Bee slipped down his thin black sock and exposed his bare foot. He knew that no one could *see* them, but he suddenly felt as vulnerable as if he had been stripped completely naked.

Bee's thumb slid into the center of Jessie's arch. The devil worked it back and forth, his other hand joining to massage Jessie's toes. He bent his head and released a stream of breath onto the sole, trailing it up and then dragging his tongue over the calloused pads. His tongue was hot, like Jessie was dipping his toes into boiling water. His foot jerked back, but Bee kept his tight hold. The devil chose his target and slid his tongue into the empty space, isolating the smallest toe. He circled his tongue around it and pulled it into his mouth, sucking, nibbling with his pointed canine.

Jessie closed his eyes. He wrapped his free leg around the stool's base and anchored himself there, worried that he might fall over, otherwise.

Then, there was pain. It shot up his leg and set his knee on fire. Jessie cried out, as surprised as he was hurt, and tried to pull his foot back again. Bee's hands squeezed Jessie's ankle and clamped down against the back of his calf, holding him in place. Jessie opened his eyes, but he could not see past the sheet of white agony that had slid over his vision. There was another wave of pain, and he didn't even realize what was happening until he heard Bee's teeth clack together, and he felt a bone snap.

His vision cleared, but only a little. Bee looked up at him, then, his bloody mouth open in a wide grin. Between his front teeth was Jessie's smallest pale toe. Jessie was only able to look at it for a second before the devil sucked it back into his mouth and wiped his tongue over his lips.

Jessie's whole body trembled. He could feel it, now, the localized, throbbing pain from where his toe had once been and the hot blood pouring from the stump. Bee raised Jessie's foot to his mouth once again, and every begging word in Jessie's vocabulary sprang to his mouth. He would not put it past Bee to take every single one. *'An ounce. An ounce. How much does a little toe weigh?'*

It didn't matter what he wanted to say. He couldn't choke it out. Jessie's words were a string of 'uhh's' that dribbled off his frozen tongue like saliva strings. Bee's eyes were sheltered bluebonnet lights dimmed only by his purple lenses as he dragged his tongue over the bleeding stump. His tongue was hotter than it had ever been before. It stung like an iron, and it seared Jessie's flesh so that it crackled at the touch. The smell of burning meat and the pain sent vomit surging up Jessie's throat, but he swallowed it down. Bee's tongue cauterized the wound, and when his work was done he released Jessie's foot to let it dangle.

"Are you in pain?" Bee asked, dragging his thumb over his bloody chin.

"Yes!" Jessie snarled. "God. Fuck. What do you think?"

Bee shrugged. "Shall I make it go away?" He touched the sides of his glasses. Jessie knew what would come next— those morphine eyes, that numb feeling that crept over every nerve and made him feel like he was dead.

"No!" Jessie stood up. Pain shot through his leg again as his foot collided with the floor, but he grit his teeth and bore it. "No, fuck—and fuck you, shit!"

"That's right, dear," Bee said. "Use all your words."

"I need..." Jessie did not know what he needed. Pain eclipsed all his senses. "I need water."

Bee stood up. He smacked his hand down on the bar counter, but Jessie was too overwhelmed to look and see where the water was coming from. He hunched over his knees and buried his face in his hands, digging his fingernails into his temples to try and redirect some of the sensation. It helped a little bit. The pain in his foot faded out into a dull throb. He felt a cold, wet glass nudge his fingers and he peeled his hand away from his temple to accept it.

The water tasted slightly metallic, but he drank half of it down anyway. Jessie shivered and held the glass against his forehead, trying to collect himself. Bee's hand slid across his back, rubbing him like he was a child in need of soothing.

Jessie pushed his tongue against the back of his teeth. "I have to go," he said. His words still sounded slurred to his own ears and his hand had already started trembling again—he was not sure how long he could hang on to the cup—but he could not stay, either. Every nerve in his body screamed against it.

"Where are you going to go, hm?" Bee didn't sound like he was fighting it, more like he was genuinely curious as to where Jessie thought he would be safe.

"Dunno." Jessie held the glass of water out. No one took it, so he let it drop. It hit the carpeted floor with a *'thunk'* but did not break. "I can't do this."

The unspoken *'you don't have a choice'* hung in the air between them. Bee did not even need to say it for them to both understand. He continued making small circles across Jessie's back, trailing his fingertips over the ridges of his spine through his clothes.

"I will come find you," Bee said, "wherever you go."

Jessie swallowed and hunched back over, rubbing his hands over his face as if the motion alone could clear his head. Bee's words served their purpose—a solemn promise and a quiet threat. Words that might be tenderly exchanged between lovers with soft intention were made cold and menacing by his tongue.

"I need..." Jessie did not know what he needed. The rest of his words fell away, neglected and unimportant. The devil did not care what it was, even if Jessie knew the right way to say it. Jessie pushed himself up from his seat. His foot screamed at him again, but it was a pain he could bear. He shoved it back into his shoe, despite the walls of the narrow toe pressing up against the wound. The front doors were visible from the bar, and he just kept walking.

It was hours, probably, or an eternity before he reached it. By that time he was dragging his hurt foot along on its side, desperate to avoid putting more pressure on it than he had to.

He didn't know if Bee was following him, and he didn't care. The simmering swamp air welcomed him as he left the casino behind.

CHAPTER FIVE

STARS THAT SHINE
IN THE DARK

"Hey, are you alright?"

The concerned voice, steeped deep in its Louisiana accent, was enough to pull Jessie from his haze. He raised his head from where he had been resting it against the side of a brick building, unsure of how long he had been leaning in that position.

"I'm fine," Jessie muttered. His eyes didn't want to focus. He blinked a few times and slid his hands into his pockets, twisting up on the lining. "I'm just...tired."

His vision slowly came together until he could see well enough to make out a vaguely familiar face. The man standing in front of him was a brassy blonde with eyes the same dull gray as a rain puddle. His bright pink polo still had his name tag clipped to the front. It said *'Leslie'*.

"Oh." Jessie rolled his shoulders to try and push himself up from the wall. A spike of pain shot up from his foot, but he tried to keep it off his face. "You work at the diner."

"Yeah, every day of my life." Leslie narrowed his eyes. "You don't look so good. Is there someone I can call? Do you need a doctor?"

"No," Jessie said. "I mean, I don't need a doctor. There isn't anyone."

"Okay." Leslie glanced over his shoulder. The busy street behind them was flooded with too much light, but the alley Jessie had stumbled into was properly dark. "Do you have somewhere to go?"

"Yes," Jessie said. "I'm fine. Really."

"Yeah," Leslie scoffed. "You look fine." He sucked on his teeth and glanced down. "I live just one building over," he said. "It's not a long walk. Are you sure you don't need somewhere to stay?"

Jessie almost refused him, but his pride stuck in his throat when he tried to shift on his feet again. He hissed through his teeth and brought his injured foot up off the ground, resting his heel against the brick wall behind him. "Maybe," he relented a little. "Just for an hour or two."

"Sure thing." Leslie moved his arm and bumped something against Jessie's hand. Jessie looked down to see the smooth black handle of a pink aluminum cane being offered to him.

"What's that?" Jessie asked, even though he knew *what* it was. He was still processing the gesture.

"It's my cane," Leslie snorted softly. "You can use it. It's only a few steps and you need it more than I do."

"Oh." Jessie wrapped his fingers around the handle. "Thanks." It was a little tall for him, but he could handle it for a few steps. He had never used a cane before and didn't know how, and it hurt his hand to lean a little too heavily on the grip.

"Here," Leslie said. "Let me show you." He took it back long enough to model the proper stance. "Hold it on the side opposite of the one that hurts. Now, lead with this leg..." He took a few steps down the alleyway and then came back. Before handing the cane back to Jessie, he adjusted the height so that it rested right near his hip. "There. We'll go slow."

Jessie didn't say anything, but he accepted the cane back with a nod. He followed Leslie out onto the sidewalk, keeping his eyes fixed straight ahead to avoid the faces of any strangers who might cast a look in his direction. He didn't want to know what they were thinking. He didn't want to see pity, concern, or disgust in anyone's eyes when he walked by. He didn't know what he hated more—the fact that using the cane helped, or the fact that the corners of Leslie's gray eyes seemed to crinkle with understanding when they stopped and he let them into the apartment building.

It was a shithole place from the outset. The stairwell had that particular smell that only concrete dust and mold could curate. The gold letter on Leslie's apartment door was corroded so that it was more green than gold, and the wood was so warped that it took a few tugs for him to get the door completely open even after it had been unlocked. The weather stripping dragged in one long piece, barely attached, as it swung.

"Home sweet home," Leslie said, with the air of someone who was too poor to be embarrassed. "Go on in."

Jessie obliged, stepping over the rotten threshold and onto the dull beige carpet. He stood around awkwardly for a minute, holding out the cane until Leslie took it and propped it up in a corner.

"Sit down anywhere you like," Leslie said. "I'm afraid I don't have much, but I can order us something." He started walking further into the apartment and stripped off his polo in the same motion. The white tank top he was wearing underneath rolled up and nearly came off with it, but he pulled it down, and for the split-second in-between Jessie caught a glimpse of silver nipple rings and forgot how to breathe.

"I'm not really hungry," Jessie said. "I can't be here long anyway." Bee *would* come looking for him, and it would not be fair to stick someone so kind in the crossfire. "But...thank you. I really appreciate it." He sat down in a dark blue recliner that looked like it was on its last leg. It wobbled as he landed, and he gripped the plush arms.

Leslie granted him a tired smile. "Yeah," he said. "Me neither, really." He dragged his hand along the back of his neck, looking for a moment like he was mulling something over. "Do you want something to change into, at least? You can't be comfortable."

He wasn't, and his suit was undoubtedly ruined. He had been sweating for hours and he had ripped off the top three buttons just trying to breathe. "You won't get it back," he warned.

"That's fine." Leslie made a beeline for his bedroom. "I've got something you can have." Even after he disappeared, he kept talking. "Are you sure about the whole not needing a doctor thing?"

"Yeah," Jessie said grimly. "The problem is pretty much taken care of—it just hurts."

"I bet," Leslie said. "What happened? If you don't mind me asking."

"Uh." Jessie looked up at the water-stained ceiling. "I tripped on a grate and broke my toe."

"Goddamn!" Leslie called from the other room. "Grates will get you every time, they're really dangerous in some areas. What do we pay taxes for? Makes sense, though, I guess there isn't anything a doctor could do." He finally re-emerged with a pair of gray sweatpants and a black t-shirt slung over his arm. "Here, you can have these," he said. "Do you need any help...?"

"No." Jessie stood quickly, sucking a curse through his teeth. "Although if you have anything for pain, I'll take that."

"I'll see what I've got," Leslie said.

That was good enough for him. Jessie gave himself a split second to consider his modesty before deciding he didn't care enough to try and walk all the way to the bathroom. He stripped his suit away in the living room, tearing off the rest of the buttons of his dress shirt and throwing it all into a pile on the floor. He sat down to take off his shoes. The inside of his Oxfords were damp with sweat, but at least he had not bled after Bee cauterized the wound. His foot was swollen near the ugly stump, but it did not look as bad as it felt—or maybe he was just being delusional. He slipped on a pair of socks anyway, just to hide the red puffiness.

Leslie reappeared a few moments later. He kicked the lump of ruined clothes aside before offering Jessie a round white pill and a cup of water.

"It's the last of what they gave me after I hurt my back a few months ago," he said. "You're welcome to it. I'm out of regular painkillers but I'll pick some up tomorrow."

Jessie popped the pill onto his tongue and then chased it down with the water. "I can't stay," he said.

"Well, if you do," Leslie did not seem too sold on that, "then I'll get some in the morning."

Jessie nodded and sat back down. Despite trying his best to settle carefully, the chair still rocked backward and knocked against the wall—striking a black mark where it had done so many times before.

Leslie's mouth quirked and he set the cup of water down on a low table.

"If you need anything, I'll be in my room," he said. "And if you leave or anything, just try to let me know so I can lock the door behind you. Otherwise, it will blow open on its own."

"Sounds safe," Jessie said.

"Trust me," Leslie snorted, "I love it here."

Three days went by without any sign of Bee. Jessie knew better than to let his guard down, but with each one that crept past, it became surprisingly difficult to resist. Most of that was due to Leslie—he was a different person once the uniform came off. He made the best French toast that Jessie had ever tasted, and he smiled a lot more when he wasn't behind a diner counter. He walked around without his shirt a lot—sometimes wearing just a thin muscle tank top that suctioned itself to his nipple piercings and gave daring flashes of his sharp hips.

He was considerate and easygoing, the opposite of Bee in every way. It wasn't fair comparing a housecat to a panther, but at the end of the day, Jessie couldn't help himself. Even for the few precious, collective hours he managed to push the devil to the back of his mind, thoughts of Bee kept popping back up like mushrooms on a rotted log.

Although with Leslie just a few inches away on the couch, it was easy for Jessie to redirect his anxiety, however temporarily. The blonde had drawn up one leg so that his bent knee was resting against the side of Jessie's thigh—the most they had touched, but Jessie didn't mind it at all. If anything, he was preoccupied with thoughts of how much closer he could get, and not paying the least bit of attention to the endless list of movies that Leslie was scrolling through.

"We are getting to the bottom of the barrel," Leslie said. "These are all from the 80's."

"Which means they are actually good." Jessie shifted in his seat, nudging Leslie's knee with his thigh. "A scary movie isn't worth anything if the blood wasn't bought at a Halloween store."

Leslie laughed. "You're wrong," he said, "but if you're the expert, maybe you want to pick."

"No," Jessie said, "but thanks."

Leslie clicked through a few more rows. "We've been on this for twenty minutes," he said. "Maybe we should think of something else to do."

"Like what?" Jessie's thoughts were solely on the wide band of Leslie's boxers that was in the process of being revealed by the gradual slide of his dark gray sweatpants. He was trying not to stare too hard. If the blonde noticed, he didn't say anything.

"Rob a liquor store? I don't know." Leslie tossed down the remote and then turned around, sliding his legs over Jessie's lap and stretching out across the couch. His shirt rode up his stomach and the open sides revealed a glimpse of the pale pink scar that ran across his chest. "I worked a double today, I shouldn't be expected to make choices."

"Oh, I see." Jessie settled his hand on Leslie's ankles, massaging the sore joints until the other man groaned. "Well, I've only ever made a few decisions—"

"A few decisions? Ever?"

"Yes, and they've all been bad ones."

"I'm not surprised, considering," Leslie said. "Although it's never too late to turn your life around."

"So you say." Jessie continued massaging up the other man's leg, feeling a bit more comfortable with the back-and-forth conversation. "I don't think there is much about my recent choices that could be considered redeemable."

The corners of Leslie's eyes crinkled. "Are we still talking about movies?" He pushed his foot down between Jessie's legs, brushing his toes over the strained seam stretched over his crotch. His touch sent a pulse of heat up to Jessie's belly, followed by a few seconds of unsteady silence as they measured each other's reactions.

Leslie was searching his face for something, but Jessie couldn't quite meet his eyes. He felt the blonde's searing gray graze like a bug trapped under a magnifying glass. Jessie drew in a shaky breath and slid his hand over Leslie's foot, arching his hips so that he pressed against it. Leslie's smile spread and he sat up, moving a little bit closer as he reached up to brush his fingers over Jessie's cheek. Jessie turned and leaned into his hand, measuring the distance between himself and those soft pink lips.

It was a gamble, but he had acquired a taste for gambling. He closed the distance between them and stole a kiss. Leslie responded immediately, enthusiastically, by parting his lips slightly and flickering his tongue out to tease Jessie's bottom lip. Jessie smiled against his mouth and met Leslie's tongue with his own, deepening the kiss as he slipped his hands through the open sides of the blonde's shirt. Leslie's skin was warm and smooth, and he shivered when Jessie's cold hands traced their way along his sides and up his back. Jessie raked his nails down, lightly, over Leslie's shoulder-blades and drew him even closer.

He did not want to think about Bee, but it was impossible not to. Jessie tried to drive the thoughts away by pressing his mouth against Leslie's throat and taking in a mouthful of flesh. He traced his tongue over the mound, sucking as he went. Leslie moaned and gripped Jessie's shirt, trying to tug it off by pulling it up over his shoulders. Jessie pulled himself back long enough to help him out, stripping off his shirt and tossing it onto the floor. Leslie's tank top came off and Jessie put his hands on the blonde's waist, kissing down his shoulders to his scarred chest, flicking the steel rings that were strung through his nipples. Leslie gasped and Jessie traced his nipples with his tongue, paying special attention to each one until they were both erect and glistening. Leslie rolled his hips and grabbed Jessie's curls, pulling him in for another heated kiss.

Another flash of Bee's face, followed by the memory of Jessie's hands against his chest, of his nails digging into that searing hot skin. Jessie drowned it out with a growl. He splayed his fingers across Leslie's chest and pushed down insistently. Leslie took the hint and laid back, stretching out as he had been before with his head just touching the arm of the couch. Jessie worked his gray sweatpants down his hips, kissing every new inch of exposed skin until they came off completely. Leslie's boxers came next, following the sweatpants' trajectory to the floor. Leslie spread his legs as far as he could and Jessie put himself between them, grasping the blonde's narrow hips and kneading his ass while pressing his mouth against the inside of his thigh.

Leslie cried out, squirming underneath him as Jessie found a tender spot and bit down. Jessie sank his teeth into the salty skin and sucked hard enough that when he pulled back, there was a dark purple mark in the center of a white impression of his teeth.

He did the same to the other thigh, burying his face in the space right where it joined with Leslie's hip and bit down again. Leslie's breath was coming out in short, needy gasps and he kept pushing his fingers through Jessie's hair, dragging his nails over his scalp and tugging on the strands.

Jessie finally unlatched from where he had been sucking and allowed his fingers to wander. He explored the expanse of trimmed, curling blonde hair that framed his prize, resting pink and glistening in the center. He slipped his fingers up and down the darkest part of Leslie's cunt, collecting the thick, clear enthusiasm on the very tips. He slid one finger up, swirling it over the man's large, ready clit. A few strokes were all it took to make the blonde whimper. Jessie smiled and glanced up, taking in the landscape of Leslie's ready, outstretched body and his pink, flushed face. Jessie lowered his head and pursed his lips, sending a stream of warm breath over Leslie's quivering thighs before touching the very tip of his tongue to his clit.

"Do you want it?" Jessie purred. Leslie whimpered again.

"Yes," he said, his throat convulsing with a hard swallow. "God—get down there."

Jessie laughed softly. He looped his arms around Leslie's thighs and pushed his face all the way down. He pressed his mouth against Leslie's soft, soaked cunt and pushed his tongue inside. Leslie moaned and placed both hands against Jessie's head, holding him down. It was a little hard to breathe that way, but Jessie didn't mind. He dragged his tongue up the entirety of Leslie's cunt, settling against his clit and teasing it with a few strokes. Leslie writhed underneath him, bucking against his face and digging his nails into Jessie's scalp. Jessie drew his clit into his mouth, sucking on it hard enough that his own tongue felt numb. Leslie's cries climbed three octaves while Jessie sucked on him, twirling his tongue around the head, teasing it and prodding it before finally releasing. Leslie's hips fell back against the couch, but Jessie was not finished. He pulled one of his arms around to put his fingers back into play. He stroked Leslie's entrance, using only two fingertips to taunt him before sliding them inside. Leslie stretched wide around his fingers, and Jessie twisted them around inside. He used his entire hand to thrust them back and forth while returning to his previous business of sucking on the blonde's clit. His fingers were coated, even the ones that were not inside. His chin was drenched and he used it to add friction, moving his face side to side and burying himself between Leslie's legs.

The blonde's thighs tightened around his head. Leslie pushed down even harder to where Jessie absolutely could not breathe. Stars began to burst across his vision, but it was worth it. He kept his tongue and fingers working in tandem, seeking out that rush, that perfect trigger.

"I'm close." Leslie's voice sounded strained. "Fuck, that feels good. Shit—I'm close!"

Jessie couldn't speak, but he let his pleasure rumble in his throat to make sure Leslie knew he was enjoying himself just as much. Leslie rocked against his face and wrapped his legs around Jessie's shoulders. His heels hit Jessie's back as he crossed his legs behind his head and kept screaming.

"Oh fuck, oh fuck, oh fuck—!"

Leslie's orgasm gushed onto Jessie's fingers. He kept thrusting and sucking until the blonde's hips started to relax. Leslie's entire body shivered and his legs fell away. Jessie finally pulled back enough to take a deep breath and then sit up, dragging his arm over his chin to wipe it clean.

"Goddamn," Leslie said. He put his hands over his face and dragged them up into his hairline.

"Was that good?" Jessie asked.

"Uhm, yes." Leslie sat up. "Yes, that was—amazing. Are you going to let me do you?"

Jessie raised a dark brow. "Me?" he asked.

"Yeah." Leslie grabbed him by the chin and kissed him. "Come over to my bedroom. I'll show you what I've got."

It was only a few steps, although Jessie's foot was still sore. He kept his hand on the wall and followed Leslie to the bedroom.

The full-size bed took up most of the space. It rested in a low wooden frame that had, at some point, been stained blue. There were drawers in the headboard and Leslie hopped onto the bed to open one of them. He pulled out a hefty blue strap-on dildo and a tangled leather harness, holding them up for approval.

"Are you into this?" Leslie asked.

Jessie leaned against the doorframe, grinning.

"Hell yes," he said. "What do you take me for?"

Leslie laughed. "Come here." He patted the bed. Jessie did as he was told, walking over to the bed and throwing himself down into the center. Jessie grabbed the band of his pants and wiggled out of them, kicking them onto the floor. Leslie took a few moments to adjust himself, slipping on the harness with practiced ease before securing the dildo in the center. He grabbed the base and then moved it around to make sure it was secure before crawling over Jessie's sprawled-out frame and claiming a kiss.

It was unbearably hot, being beneath Leslie with the strap-on hanging between his legs. Jessie was already wet and aching with need. He spread his legs and pulled up his knees, inviting Leslie between them, reaching up to slide his hands over the blonde's beautiful shoulders.

"Oh, shit," Jessie moaned against Leslie's mouth. "I need you to fuck me."

"Patience," Leslie teased, grabbing the dildo and placing the silicone head against Jessie's cunt. He stroked it up and down. To Jessie, it was *audible* how wet he was.

"I'm not patient," Jessie said. He set his mouth against one of the dark marks he left on Leslie's neck, sucking on it again while he dragged his nails over the blonde's shoulders. He left pink trails in their wake, and Leslie hissed before lowering his hips.

Jessie plunged his hand down to help. He grabbed hold of the dildo and made sure that it was pointed in the right direct while Leslie sank down. The heavy, thick dildo slid right inside, stretching him open until he ached. Jessie could not stop the moan that shivered up his throat as he clung to Leslie, spreading his legs as wide as they could go so that he felt every stroke. Leslie settled against him, and his hips rolled in rhythmic thrusts. Jessie's eyes rolled up and he reached back to grab the headboard, clawing at the old wood in an attempt to find anything he could hang onto. The bed rocked underneath him, and if there were any lingering thoughts of Bee, they were driven out with every hard, deep thrust. His mouth fell open, but the only sounds that came out were feral and needy.

"Harder," he managed to groan, "fuck me harder!"

Leslie picked up speed. He drove his hands down into the bed on either side of Jessie and drove his hips down as hard as he could. Sweat beaded on his forehead and he swept his damp blonde hair back. Jessie kissed him again, every muscle tightening as he fought to reach that blessed high. His orgasm was right within reach. It dangled in front of him, perversely elusive.

"Harder!" His throat was dry. His voice sounded raw. Leslie pulled his hips back, only long enough to detach the strap-on from its harness. He placed the dildo, hot and slick, back between Jessie's legs and used his hand to thrust. His hands worked faster and harder than his hips, and Jessie grabbed a pillow to pull over his face. His thighs shook and Leslie used his free hand to grab onto his knee, keeping his legs spread while fucking him so hard that his whole vision swam, even behind his closed eyes.

"Fuck!" Jessie screamed, ripping away the pillow and throwing his arms above his head. His hands banged against the headboard, but he was too close to cumming to feel any pain. "Fuck, fuck, fuck me! Yes! Fuck me! Shit!" He brought his thighs together, squeezing Leslie's hand and the dildo between his legs as he came. His orgasm spiked through him and made his cunt clench. Leslie rocked the dildo back and forth as much as he could with Jessie's thighs squeezing him, letting Jessie ride it out until his pleasure had been found. Jessie finally nodded, making a vague gesture that he hoped could be interpreted as 'enough'. Leslie slid the dildo out and tossed it to the side of the bed while Jessie slid his hands into his hair, dragging them back down his face and exhaling sharply.

"Wow," he said. "How do you feel?"

"Great." Leslie collapsed beside him. "How do you feel?"

"Like a new man," Jessie said, staring up at the roof. "I don't think I could move if I wanted to."

"Great news, you don't have to." Leslie picked up the corner of a rogue blanket. "After all that, I think it would be wrong to make you keep sleeping on the couch."

Jessie laughed, too tired to argue, and turned onto his side. Leslie cuddled up close to him, tracing his fingers down Jessie's side and over his hip.

"What do your tattoo say?" Leslie asked. His fingers made little circles over Jessie's thigh.

Jessie shifted and put his hand underneath his head, not pulling his eyes away from the wall. "It says *the devil will make me a free man*," he said.

"Oh," Leslie said. "Interesting." He lingered over it just a minute before pulling the blanket all the way up until they were both covered. He wrapped his arm around Jessie's chest, and within seconds, Jessie was out cold.

CHAPTER SIX

WITH HIS ARMS FOLDED UP AND HIS BLUE EYES CLOSED

It was the smell of cigar smoke that pulled Jessie out of a dead sleep. It made the back of his throat tingle and he sat up to cough, doing his best to smother the sound so that he did not wake up the other person in the bed. His head spun as he rose. In the pitch-black bedroom, the only thing he could see was a glowing orange circle with trails of white smoke licking at its crumpled edges. And in the perfect silence, it was even possible to hear the crackle of burning tobacco.

"Bee." The word escaped Jessie's lips so quietly that it could barely be heard. Something else appeared in the darkness, then, a flash of a pointed gold canine with a tip like a knife.

"Jessie," Bee's voice was slick like oil being rubbed all over his skin. "I told you that I would come find you."

Jessie's swallow got stuck at the back of his throat. "Took you long enough," he said. His words came out garbled, and he dragged his fingers nervously underneath his nose. He couldn't tell if he was bleeding, but his nostrils burned and his knuckles came back slick. "I was starting to think you had given up on me."

"Oh, no," Bee said. "Not ever." Another cloud of cigar smoke followed his words. Jessie's vision was adjusting to the darkness, and he could just make out those blazing blue eyes—although it looked like there were more than just the two of them. He counted six fuzzy, floating pairs that clustered around the shadow of Bee's head. Jessie blinked and his eyes squelched like there were bubbles trapped under his lids.

"Should I...?" Jessie was distracted by a tickle on his upper lip. Thin blood mixed with salty sweat pooled in the separation between his lips and made the raw bottom sting. "Do you want me to stand up?"

"Can you?" Bee asked. "How is your foot?"

"It's fine." Jessie's squeezed his own wrist just to see if his heart was actually beating as quickly as it seemed. "I can manage—"

"Who is the guy?" Bee cut him off. Another cloud of smoke made Jessie cough again. Blood that was running down to his chin sprayed from his mouth and speckled the hand he held up as cover.

"No one," Jessie said. He turned his head and spit blood onto the floor.

"No one? He's got your juices all over his dildo." Bee's words tugged on something inside of Jessie that made his whole lower half tighten. It was as if the strap-on was inside of him all over again, slick and heavy.

"It's..." Jessie's words faltered. "Please." He shivered again. "Let's just go."

"Fine by me." Bee tapped the end of his cigar. A few glowing embers fell to the floor. "I'm sick of this place, personally. I think it's time we went home."

"Home?" Jessie dug his hands into the mattress for leverage.

"I've got two one-way tickets back to Texas," Bee said. "Sorry that your friend won't be able to come along."

Jessie did not dare glance in Leslie's direction. "I don't think you'd like him," he muttered.

"I don't think I would either," Bee agreed. "I'm more of a one-meal-at-a-time sort of devil."

The words had barely slithered out of his mouth before Leslie's entire body convulsed so hard that it shook the bed. His mouth fell open and he sputtered out a choke that left any attempt at words smothered in white foam. It came pouring out of his mouth, running down the sides of his cheeks where his veins were visible underneath his suddenly sickly, near-translucent skin. Even in the dark, Jessie could see it all clearly.

"Stop it!" He gave up on keeping his voice down and growled at Bee. "He didn't do anything to you!"

"Other than touching my things?" Bee ground out his cigar on the footboard. "That's good enough for me."

Leslie gagged again—an awful, retching sound. Blood came up with the foam and his gray eyes rolled up into his head. His back arched sharply, his chest jutting upward while his spine crackled in several places. He spasmed again, his hands flying up to claw at his throat, but they could only batter weakly against his trachea.

There was another crunch. Leslie's head bowed back far enough that his larynx protruded out like a flag. Everything was getting squeezed out through his mouth, his eyes, his nose, and his ears—clear fluid that ran until it turned cloudy and then bloody. When he fell back against the bed, he was completely still, though his eyeballs bulged out slightly more from their sockets and he was still leaking.

Jessie wanted to look away, but he forced himself to keep staring. He needed the image of Leslie seared into his brain. He needed that for his guilt, in case he ever thought it would be a smart idea to leave Bee behind again.

His nose finally stopped bleeding. Jessie sniffed and flicked off some of the crusty buildup before he stood.

There were only a few steps between him and the end of the bed. Bee waited until he had moved a little closer and then extended a hand.

"Are you ready?" the devil asked.

"It's not like I have anything to pack," Jessie scoffed. He was still naked, so he picked a pair of sweatpants and one of Leslie's tank-tops up from the floor and slid them on. They didn't fit him perfectly, but he didn't care. On their way out, he spotted the pink aluminum cane propped up by the door. Jessie groused internally over ethics for a few seconds before grabbing it by the handle and following Bee out into the hallway.

"Cute," Bee said. "I think red would suit you better."

"Maybe," Jessie shrugged, "but I might as well use this one. He doesn't need it anymore."

The flight back to Dallas felt longer than it was. There was no Dramamine to take off the edge, this time, and no Bee sitting next to him to rub his leg. Bee booked them in different seats, putting himself in first class while letting Jessie ride coach. It was unbelievably petty, and

Jessie was more bent out of shape about it than was probably warranted—but only because being alone with his thoughts and his nausea put him in his own special little corner of Hell. He was grateful to be pressed up against a window, at least. Blue skies and gathering clouds were a nice distraction. As long as he stayed focused on the blue, he wouldn't have to think about Leslie's gray eyes rolling back, or the bloody spit pouring from his quivering mouth.

As many times as he had seen Bee commit some kind of atrocity, this was the first one he felt directly responsible for. Sour guilt made his stomach roil and sent sharp stabs of pain down to his intestines. He spent most of the flight doubled over with his arms wrapped around his middle and his forehead resting against the back of the seat in front of him.

He kept his gaze fixed on the sky, though. Motion sickness was better than what waited for him whenever he closed his eyes.

Bee's car was waiting for them when they landed. It was a sleek, cherry-red thing with classic fins and a soft convertible top. The first thing he did was lower the top and latch it in place. He stroked the tan leather seats as he walked back around to the driver's side, smiling like a proud parent.

"Did you miss me?" he cooed, patting the driver's side door fondly. It sprang open for him and he slid right in, glancing over at Jessie with his hand on the steering wheel. "Well, come on," he said. "How about some breakfast?"

Jessie slid into the driver's side and dropped the pink cane into the floorboard, wedging it between his seat and the door. "Are you still mad at me?" he asked.

"Yes," Bee said. "And I probably will be until we eat."

Jessie sucked on his teeth. "There is that diner close to home," he said. "The one that fries its own donuts."

"Perfect." Bee flashed a grin. The engine purred as the car started up, and Jessie slid his fingers through the door handle in a preemptive death-grip.

Bee drove like a bat out of hell. To him, speed limits were more like scorecards.

ld Town Buzz had been around for at least as long as Jessie had been living in the state. His first memories were with his dad and getting breakfast after the long drive from Richmond. A blown tire, a pitch-black road, and a boring auto shop all led to fresh-fried donuts covered in powdered sugar at 5AM.

'We'll get there in no time,' he remembered how certain his dad sounded as he sipped drip coffee and retraced their route on a crinkled road map.

Jessie shook his head to clear out the weird memory and slid into a booth seat across from Bee. The devil had already picked up a clear plastic-covered menu and was looking it over with the same solemnity and focus that most people reserved for front-page news.

Jessie waited a few minutes, scraping his nails over the scuffed red surface of the table that separated them. "So," he finally said, "are we going to talk about it?"

"Talk about what?" Bee didn't glance up.

"All of it. The whole thing." Jessie pulled his hand back to bite his nails.

"Are you ready to hit the blackjack tables again already?" Bee smiled. "Moderation, dear."

Jessie scrunched up his brow into a scowl. "No," he said. "The other thing. This morning."

"Oh, that? No, I don't think so." Bee flipped his menu over to glance at the back. "We've already addressed that. It has been taken care of. Besides, if we start down the road of your infidelities, I am going to lose my appetite." He set the menu down and rested his elbows on the table so he could cradle his chin on his hands. "You've got a lot of learning left to do. I thought I'd made my expectations clear from the gate."

"You did." Jessie bit a nail too close to the quick and distracted himself from the dull pain by gnawing on the sides. "But then, you know, you bit off my toe."

"Jessie," the devil said, "I have given you everything you ever asked of me. I held you back from taking a fast journey up the river to oblivion. I ask very little in return—almost nothing, in fact, all things considered. Are you going to gripe with me about something so small? Something you barely even miss? What is going to be next? 'Oh, no, Mr. Devil—please don't be so dependable and attentive in the way you rock my world'." He snorted.

Jessie glared. "That doesn't sound like me."

"Yes, it does. I could drop your voice a few more octaves, but I don't think you deserve it."

Jessie pulled his hand down from his mouth and wove his fingers together, frustrated.

"My question to *you*," Bee said, tapping the side of his lavender glasses, "is do you even want this?"

"Yes." Jessie ground his teeth. "I want it just as much now as I did then. More, probably."

"Then I need you to act like it," Bee said. "If you are going to be the devil's slut, I expect you to take some goddamn pride in the label."

A red-haired waitress wearing too many artsy turquoise rings appeared at the side of the table and interrupted their conversation. Jessie kept his eyes fixed firmly on his hands while Bee placed an order for both of them—two cups of coffee, a basket of fresh donuts, and two plates of eggs with bacon. Once she was gone, he turned his attention back to

Jessie, blue eyes boring through the center of his purple lenses.

"*The devil's slut.*" Jessie rubbed his nose. "You have such a way with words."

"Tell me I'm wrong."

"A spade's a spade," Jessie said. "I don't have to like it."

"I think you like some of it." Bee paused again as the waitress brought their coffee over and set the cups down in front of them. Bee thanked her and picked up three packets of sugar from a nearby bowl, flicking them back and forth between his fingers until all the granules had collected at the bottom. "If you have complaints, Jessie-beau, I'd like to hear them."

The pet name made everything tight between his legs. Jessie clenched his thighs together and leaned over a bit, stuffing one hand down between them. "Not really," he said, "not about the sex. Is that what you mean?"

"Is it?" Bee tore the sugar packets open.

Jessie pressed his lips together, pulling the bottom one between his teeth. "Things could be better," he said. "If you are going to treat me like this I could—get more."

Bee stuck a spoon down into his coffee and smiled. "I'm listening."

"I don't know what, exactly." Jessie straightened. "We could travel more. Places that I want to go, too—like Las Vegas."

Bee's smile stretched until it was positively vicious. "Las Vegas, the city of bright lights. All right, I think we can manage that one."

"And I want..." Jessie sucked in a deep breath, "...I want the changes to happen faster. People still look at me and I feel like they know. I don't want that, anymore."

"You want to blend in completely?" Bee sipped his coffee. "There is an art to transformation, Jessie, nothing happens overnight."

"With you it does," Jessie said, a bit bitterly. "You could pull a card from your deck and make it all happen in a flash. I've seen you do more for even less of a reason. And I'm...*asking* you to do it."

Bee tilted his head, like he was thinking it over, and drummed his fingers against the side of his coffee cup. "You interest me, Jessie," he said after a minute. "You want what everyone wants, but you don't ask me for it. You want money and freedom, same as anyone—but you're still living in the same house, you don't drive, and you don't like swiping my credit cards even when you know money doesn't mean anything to me. Your furniture is old, your lifestyle is monotonous. It doesn't have to be. You asked me to transform you into *your* ideal version of yourself. I've cut deals with a lot of men like you, and you would be surprised how many take on a face and physique that needs infernal intervention to achieve. You didn't even want to swap out your equipment. You're a pain in my ass, but you haven't been hard to please."

"I'm not sure of what you're getting at," Jessie said.

"I've seen your soul, and it's as black as tar," the devil said. "I know that when I rip it from your chest it's going to stick to my fingers and drip through them like congealed oil. I'm your only friend for a reason. No one likes you because your personality is as irredeemable as your soul. You're not a good person, sweetheart, and if I speed up this process—"

"Is that what this is?" Jessie cut him off. "You're afraid that I won't need you anymore?"

"*Afraid* of nothing," Bee was quick to correct him. "I'm just not ready to give you up."

Jessie exhaled sharply through his nose. "I guess I should be flattered."

"I wouldn't go that far," Bee said. "I just don't feel like waiting around for another sucker to come along."

The redhead waitress came back balancing plates of food along her arm. Jessie's stomach grumbled at the sight of eggs with wobbling gold centers and crisp brown edges and bacon so close to being burnt that it curled in on itself while glistening with fat. He grabbed a plate without waiting and punctured an egg yolk with his fork. It bled yellow all over.

Bee seemed happy with the display of appetite. He picked up a puffy donut and ripped it in half so that steam escaped the soft, pale center.

"Can we go home after this?" Jessie asked. "I really want to shower and change my clothes."

"Sure thing, Jessie-beau," the devil said. "Anything you like." He stuffed a torn piece of donut into his mouth.

CHAPTER SEVEN

THE DEVIL WILL MAKE HIM A FREE MAN

It was never cold enough inside his bedroom, even with the drapes drawn and the air conditioner turned down as low as it could go without the coils icing over. Jessie sat on the side of his bed and stuck his foot over the grate to make sure it was actually blowing out air. He felt *something*, so he knew it was working—the feeble stream just wasn't good enough to combat the Texas sun's oppressive heat. It seeped in through the little pink house's seams and cracks, suffocating and still.

He was sweating. There was no reason for him to sweat in his own house.

It had only been a few days since New Orleans, but it already felt like a memory that belonged to someone else.

After the diner, Bee dropped off Jessie and left. He occupied the house next door, so he was never far, but it had been almost two days since Jessie had seen him. That wasn't unusual—Bee was only ever guaranteed to visit on Sundays to collect his due. The rest of the week was up to whim.

Even though things were back to normal, or what *had* been normal before New Orleans, Jessie still felt loneliness like an aggravated cavity. He had neglected it for too long, and now it festered—and there was no cure for it. He would rather sit in pain than pick up his phone and call on the devil to keep him company. He had no idea what they would do, anyway. He didn't feel like fucking. He didn't want to play blackjack at the kitchen table until the sun went down. He wanted something *else.*

He thought about Leslie again, about sitting on the couch and scrolling through an endless list of bad movies. He thought about popcorn, about root beer, about sitting on the apartment stairwell while drinking rum and soda.

His chest ached. Jessie pushed the thought into the back of his mind, attempting to grind it out against the walls of his skull. That was his method every time thoughts of Leslie came up. It hadn't worked so far, but he kept trying.

'Three days isn't long enough to get to know anyone.'

A knock on his front door startled him back into the moment. Jessie raised his head and tangled his fingers up in the cover underneath him. He leaned over to try and catch a glimpse at the front porch from his window, but he couldn't see anything through the drapes. He shifted his back teeth and waited, keeping his breathing slow and even. If he was perfectly still, and perfectly quiet, maybe they would leave. It was probably just the postman, anyway. Bee would have let himself in.

There was silence for the span of a heartbeat before the knock came again. Jessie ground his teeth together so hard that they squealed and then he launched himself off the side of the bed. Jessie caught himself on the footboard, keeping the pressure off his bad foot as he took a moment to grab his cane. He made his way to the front door, keeping his steps as slow and quiet as possible until he could press himself up against the wood and look through the peephole.

He glimpsed brown hair and tortoiseshell glasses. Jessie's heart slammed into his ribcage, knocking out a panicked breath. His fingertips squeaked as they slid down the door towards the knob and he kept staring, blinking a few times to try and make sure he was not *actually* imagining things. The person standing on the porch tilted their head back to glance at the peephole and smiled, waving.

Jessie swallowed. "It isn't possible," he muttered to himself. He considered abandoning the door and calling Bee, but that somehow seemed like a worse idea.

He had no choice. Jessie opened the door.

"Good morning." Abel Castle stood on the porch looking fresher than a daisy in a loose white blouse with a yellow chiffon scarf tied around their neck. Their nose was shielded by the shadow that was cast by their wide-brimmed hat, which was the same crisp, startling white as their shirt. They looked like they had made the decision to pop by after a very boozy brunch. "I'm glad to catch you at home."

Jessie tightened his grip on the door, taking up the entire frame with his body so that Abel couldn't just sneak past him to get inside. "What do you want?"

"May I come in?"

"Bee isn't here."

"I didn't think he was. May I come in anyway?" Abel smiled. "What is it they used to say—*be not afraid?*"

Jessie snorted but did not step aside. "How did you find me?" he asked.

"I looked you up. It wasn't difficult," Abel said.

"That isn't comforting. And it's barely an answer." Jessie looked around, suddenly nervous that Bee might sense something was amiss and come stepping through the hedges. "He will *kill* me if he finds you here."

"I will be in and out," Abel reassured him. "Besides, I am not afraid of him. You shouldn't be, either."

"I'm not sure what makes you say that." Jessie glanced across the yard again before shifting slightly closer to the door. "What do you want? You didn't answer that question."

"Just to talk." Abel spread their hands. "Is that a sin?"

Jessie rubbed his face. "This is a house of sinners." He finally moved aside enough for Abel to squeeze through. The pretty devil smiled at him and touched the brim of their straw hat in thanks as they walked in.

"What a charming place," Abel said as they stepped into the living room. "It could use a bit more light."

"I usually try to avoid letting it turn into an oven." Jessie shut the front door with his heel and followed them in. "You flew states over just to talk?"

"Well, I had hoped to catch you one last time while you were still in town to make my offer." Abel looked around for a minute before settling on the couch, crossing their legs primly and throwing their arm across its back.

"You have an offer?" Jessie sat down on an ottoman. "For what?"

"For your soul." Abel adjusted their glasses on their nose. "And yes, I know—you have already promised it to Bee." They flashed another smile. "It would be a complicated exchange, but possible."

Jessie's heart felt like it was being dragged down into the pit of his stomach. "Thanks," he said, "but no thanks. I've got enough—Bee gives me what I need. We talked about this, actually. I'm not interested."

"I know change is unpleasant," Abel said. "Although you could at least consider my counter-offer. I can do things for you that Bee cannot."

Jessie pulled his bottom lip between his teeth and chewed off a patch of dry skin. "Like what?"

"I can cut a soul loose." Abel raised their chin. "Is there, perhaps, someone you have lost recently that you might wish to have back? It gets a little lonely around here, doesn't it? You reek of guilt—not to be rude. I could smell it on you as soon as you opened the door. It's sour, like old beer. Why not rectify a wrong and do yourself a favor at the same time?"

They *knew.* Jessie could tell that they knew, even if he wasn't sure how. He dragged his palms over his knees, rubbing them back and forth as he tried to untangle the mess of words that was spilling from the devil's mouth. They weren't like Bee—not at all. Bee's words were fast and slick. They sent up sparks when they struck his tongue and he spit them out as hot as hellfire. Abel's words rolled off their tongue sweeter than molasses. They were words of wisdom coated in sugar so that the medicine went down easier. The words they used to describe Jessie's guilt were harsh, but it *sounded* tender coming from them. Concern. Pity. Jessie felt sick.

"So, what?" Jessie rubbed his fingers underneath his nose. There was no use beating around the bush. "You bring back Leslie, and then my conscience is clear? We live together happily-ever-after, is that it?"

Abel shrugged. "My offer is on the table. It is up to interpretation."

"I don't think you understand everything about the deal I have made with Bee," Jessie said shortly. "He *makes* me what I am. Can you do that? Can you keep me on the path of becoming a man?"

"There are some things Bee can do that I cannot," Abel admitted. "You will stay as you are, and nothing will change. You will not become any more or less the man you are sitting there."

Jessie's teeth tore at the inside of his cheek. It was a shabby deal, in his opinion, except for the fact that Abel was right about his guilt. He hadn't slept a full night because every time he closed his eyes, he saw Leslie vomiting foam, and he saw the lit end of Bee's cigar burning in front of a half dozen pairs of blue eyes. It never occurred to him that there might be a chance of bringing Leslie back. He didn't know how it worked, and he had a feeling he shouldn't ask.

He wasn't satisfied with his looks. He wasn't satisfied with his voice. He wanted even less of a chest and even more hair. He wanted his voice to hit the basement and he wanted his cheeks to hollow out. Some things could be achieved over time without Bee's help, but that required doctors, so many doctors, and years and money that he did not have.

Then again, it was his fault that Leslie was dead. There was a chance that he could learn to live with his current state, if it meant sleeping a full night, and not living with that on his conscience.

Jessie hunched over his knees and buried his face in his hands. Bee or Abel. What did it matter? He was damned either way. And he was food, either way.

After allowing himself a moment of despair, Jessie sat back up.

"What would be your due?" he finally asked. "What would you come to collect?"

Abel trailed their fingers through the tails of their yellow chiffon scarf.

"I'll take what Bee gets," they said. "That is what I want."

Not what he was expecting, but not what he *didn't* expect, either. "Every Sunday." He took a deep breath. "How complicated is this process?"

A little satisfied smirk tugged the corner of Abel's mouth where a sweet, kissable mole rested. "Where did you say you met Bee?"

"At a crossroads."

"We need to put you back in that place," Abel said.

Before more could be discussed, the front door opened, and Jessie flinched. He sat up even straighter on the ottoman and grabbed his cane in case he needed to stand. He couldn't defend himself, if Bee decided to come for him, but he wasn't going to be a sitting duck.

Bee stepped into the living room. His pink collared shirt was unbuttoned almost to his navel, and the sleeves were rolled up past his elbows to flaunt his structured forearms. His straight white slacks didn't have a speck of dirt on them—surprising, because he always crossed through the yard. He smelled strongly of cologne and hair pomade, like he was fresh out of the shower. He glanced over at Jessie and smiled without a shred of good nature, flashing his gold canine.

Every ring on his finger had a jewel and the gold chain around his neck sparkled like it was new. He had come with intention.

Jessie knew he would be lucky if he lived to see another dawn.

"Hail Beelzebub," Abel's voice ambled across the room, completely unfazed by the interruption. "Prince of Gluttony, Lord of Flies. How long has it been since we last crossed paths?"

"Hello Hastur." Bee hooked his thumbs onto his pockets and tilted his head. "King in Yellow, Lord of Unvarnished Truth. Not long enough. What are you doing in my house?"

Abel pursed their lips. "Here, I thought it was Jessie's house."

"Jessie is mine," Bee said, "so everything here is mine, too." As if to drive home his point, he set his hand on Jessie's shoulder and squeezed. His skin was uncomfortably hot, like the surface of a stove. Not quite enough to burn, but enough to warn.

"That seems to be up for debate." Abel switched the way their legs were crossed, tugging on their scarf. "I hear your Jessie is up for a little renegotiation of his contract."

"Is that so?" Bee dug his nails into Jessie's shoulder. They pierced right through his tank top and pricked the skin wherever the fabric wasn't. "Sounds like Jessie and I need to have a little talk. You should go—find somewhere else to scavenge for your meal."

"I don't know about that," Abel said. "It always tastes so much better off someone else's plate."

Bee snarled. It was a deep, feral sound that Jessie had never heard him make before—almost like a cornered fox.

"He has the rights to an eleventh hour," Abel went on. "If he wants to return to the crossroads, you cannot deny him that."

"But only once," Bee reminded them. "Most people choose to hold onto that hand."

"Better offers don't come along, for most people." Abel shrugged. "Anyway, that is Jessie's choice to make."

Suddenly, Jessie could feel both pairs of eyes bearing down on him. He squirmed on the ottoman, rubbing his hand nervously across his nose.

"What happens with the eleventh hour?" Jessie asked, trying to keep his own voice steady.

"You can keep the contract that we have," Bee said, "or you can choose another. Most people, like I said, choose to play that hand when they are close to death. You could make a plea for redemption and save your own soul. I've seen it happen more times than I can count."

"So..." Jessie looked up at him. "You aren't even guaranteed anything at the end? I could plead for salvation and my soul could be purified—and you get nothing? This is all a gamble?"

"Everything is a gamble, but it is worth it," Bee said. "I always win more rounds than I lose."

"And redemption is not on the table, here," Abel added. "Your soul will be damned without chance of reprieve."

"Right," Bee said. "You don't get to do it again. No take-backsies, as they say."

"And if I choose Abel—Hastur's contract—" Jessie stumbled a bit over the names, "then what?"

Bee thinned his lips. "I can't do anything to you," he said. "Rules of the game."

"He might be a sore loser," Abel said, "but he will bow out nonetheless."

"And *you.*" Bee turned his harrowing gaze back to Abel. "If he doesn't choose *you,* then you get lost. I don't want to see you again until the saints come marching in. Capiche?"

Abel pushed their glasses up the bridge of their nose. "Agreed," they said. "Although I think you underestimate your Jessie."

"You say that. I think I give him too much credit." Bee slammed his hand into the center of Jessie's back. "If we are going to do this, we are doing it proper. Come on, Jessie-beau."

"Is it the same crossroads?" Jessie stood up. His palms were so sweaty that they slid over the silicone head of his cane.

"Not quite," Bee said. "It doesn't work like that, when you have to go back to it. Things don't ever shake out the same way twice. I guess our royal hotshot didn't explain it to you, did they?"

"No," Jessie said. "What is going to happen?"

"You will find out when we get there, won't you? One way or the other." Bee and Abel exchanged a private look.

"There is a lovely oak just a few miles up the road," Abel suggested. "With nothing else surrounding it."

"That will do fine," Bee said.

"Are we taking your car?" Jessie asked.

"Fuck no," Bee snorted. "They even made *Jesus* walk."

CHAPTER EIGHT

HIS ELEVENTH HOUR

The shade of the enormous oak tree stretched across the dry, patchy grass for what seemed like a mile. Its gnarled branches twisted out in every direction, sprouting smaller branches like endless nerves threading through one another bearing wide leaves and weighed down by acorns. Jessie stepped over the shells as he walked—the ground was littered with them. His legs shook from the exertion of the long, hot walk and his bad foot throbbed. His hand was sore, too, from leaning on the cane so heavily for the last half mile.

Neither Abel nor Bee seemed to be suffering. There wasn't a drop of sweat between the two of them, although they had been talking almost since they started down the road. They went back and forth in a language that Jessie didn't understand, although their affected Southern accents were still jarringly present.

The oak was far enough from the road that Jessie couldn't even see it from where he was standing. Bee was looking up in the branches, inspecting them as if he was searching for something. Abel waited, drumming their light fingers against the crook of their elbow.

Finally, Bee wagged his fingers and gestured for Jessie to walk over. "Come here," Bee said. "I think this spot will do."

Jessie made his way obediently towards the devil. When he approached Bee, he saw that there was a short brown stool set on top of a bulging root. His eyes climbed upward, following the path of Bee's hand as the devil grabbed hold of a noose that was swinging only inches above his head. Jessie's mouth fell open, but his words were gone. He raised one hand instinctively to press against his throat, dragging his fingertips over his blooming Adam's apple.

"I don't understand," he finally managed to speak, but the words came out faint.

"I suppose in this case, the crossroads is more metaphorical than anything," Abel was kind enough to explain. "It is not enough to be presented with a choice. You must be put in a position of desperation at least somewhat similar to where you were when this all began."

"You wanted to die," Bee said. "You were so close to death that your heels were burning as you walked by." He smiled fondly with the memory. "I just held out my hand and pulled you back from the ledge. No ledge, no deal—so we have to put you back."

"This is insane." Jessie tried to take a step back, but Bee grabbed his arm.

"*You* wanted this," the devil reminded him. "This is your Eleventh Hour."

"Not to be squandered." Abel moved to stand on one side of the stool. "Choose wisely."

"And no promises that I won't kick the fucking thing out from under you if you don't," Bee said. He pulled Jessie over until there was no other choice than to step up onto the stool. It wobbled a bit underneath him. Jessie thought he was going to be sick. Bee grabbed the rope and pulled it down until the noose slipped over Jessie's head and pulled it snugly around his neck. The rope was rough and its harsh fibers dug into his skin. Tears sprang to Jessie's eyes as his heart started to race. He refused to cry and closed his eyes to keep them back, but he could do nothing for his heart.

"Do you need to be reminded of my offer?" Abel asked.

Jessie shook his head. He did not even trust himself to speak.

He took another deep breath that shook his entire body. The tears sank back down, nestled back into his ducts, ready to spring at a moment's notice but quieted for the time being. Jessie opened his eyes again, slowly, and found himself staring at the overhanging branches of the oak tree in front of him. A slight breeze came, just enough to make them stir, and he watched a few more acorns fall to the ground. He couldn't see Bee anymore, or Abel. He knew that they were standing on either side of him and he could still smell Bee's cologne. It was all different now, somehow. The sun filtering through the branches was more golden and beautiful than he had ever seen it before. He couldn't believe how long it had been since he had found himself laying underneath an oak tree, or any tree—staring up through the branches for glimpses of the blue sky on the other side. He had done so much of that, as a kid, back in Virginia when his grandmother still had the apple blossom tree in her front yard. Things were simpler, then. Much simpler.

He knew what his choice would be before he even felt the noose tighten, but he dreaded speaking it out loud. There was nothing wrong with taking a few moments, regardless, to enjoy the sunshine and the absolute stillness. It was more peace than he had felt in a long time.

He thought about Leslie—about how pretty the sunlight would look on his blonde hair. Three days wasn't long enough to know anyone, but it was long enough to notice small things—like the freckles on their shoulders and nose that only darkened whenever the sun hit them. Or like the little white scars on their fingers from one too many slipped boxcutters and cardboard edges. It was enough to notice the callouses on their heels and the odd way their wrist popped from where it had never quite healed from an injury. Leslie, he thought, was very miserably human. He lived and he toiled like everyone else. The only remarkable thing about him had been the circumstances of his death.

Jessie, on the other hand, was also miserably human— but his life was *different*. He had grown so used to having Bee around that he had become almost numb to his presence, but there really wasn't anything *usual* about their relationship at all.

Did he feel guilty because he was responsible for Leslie's death, or was he simply rattled by what Leslie represented?

After all, without Bee, Jessie would be living a similar life—or even less of one, if he was being honest with himself. Leslie put every penny he had towards surviving. He had medical bills through the nose—Jessie had seen them piling up on the kitchen counter, ignored. He died alone, as far as anyone knew, and Jessie doubted that there had even been much of a stir made about it.

Why waste a wish righting a wrong, when the only wrong that had been done was in doubting his own choice? Eleventh Hour be damned.

'Eleventh Hour be damned,' he thought to himself.

Jessie brushed his fingers over his jeans where his tattoo lay underneath.

'The devil will make me a free man', it said.

"Damn me, too," he muttered aloud. "Until the saints come marching in."

Jessie wrapped his fingers around the noose and gave it a tug. It didn't come loose, at first, and panic quickened his heartbeat once again. Warm hands touched his neck and stroked his jaw as they worked the noose free. The rope finally slackened, and Jessie drew in a deep sigh of relief. His knees shook again, and the stool wobbled.

If he was lucky, he wouldn't throw up.

"Come on down, Jessie-beau." Bee extended his hand. "All you have to do is say my name."

Jessie looked down and met the devil's eyes. Texas bluebonnets lost in a field of lavender. Jessie could almost see his own face reflected in those merciless purple lenses.

"Bee," the name came out, worn and tired, dragged across his vocal cords. "Can we go home?"

"Sure thing, Jessie-beau." Bee wrapped his arm around Jessie's shoulders and threw a glance at Abel.

For the first time since Jessie had met them, Abel looked bored. They trailed their fingers through the air flippantly, as if brushing aside the entire situation. "Not really what I expected," they said. "I suppose you can be quite convincing when you want to be."

"One of my many talents," Bee said. "Now you hold up your end."

"Of course," Abel said. "I'm out of here." They gave Jessie one last long, lingering look. "Take care of that bitter soul of yours," they said. "It's going to make one hell of a meal, someday."

Jessie stared. He had nothing to say in response. They did not seem to expect one, they simply flashed all their teeth in a smile and then walked away from the old oak.

It took more than half the day to walk back. Orange sunset spread across the sky like a wildfire and bathed Jessie's small pink house in daunting, wicked light. Bee sprinted the last few steps that led up to the porch and opened up the door, even though Jessie remembered locking it distinctly, and the devil didn't use a key.

"Are you going home tonight?" Jessie asked without looking at him. They hadn't said much to each other on the walk back. Jessie had, in truth, been afraid to ask too much. He wasn't sure he wanted any answers just yet.

"This is my house too," Bee said, echoing back what he had said to Abel. "Everything in it belongs to me."

Jessie swallowed. "I will make it up to you," he said. "I don't want you to think that I am—ungrateful."

"Oh, I know you are," Bee said. "You're an ungrateful bastard who has never appreciated a damn thing I've ever done for you. That's never been a question. I hope you didn't think that I was going to let you off the hook, either, for that little display. Inviting Hastur, for one thing, the King in Yellow into your house—I didn't think even you would be that stupid, Jessie-beau."

Jessie grabbed the back of a kitchen chair and pulled it out so that he could collapse. "Well," he said dryly, "I didn't know they were a king—or lord, or whatever. You called them about two or three different things."

"They're a pain in the ass, is what they are." Bee opened the fridge and pulled out two bottles of root beer by their necks. "And a downright vulture—thinking they can swoop in and steal *my* feast."

Jessie wrinkled his nose. "Would you really have let them?"

"Don't start with that." Bee popped the metal tops off the bottles and sat down before passing one to Jessie. "Your choices are your own. Just because I knew you would stick with me doesn't mean that I'm not irritated by the inconvenience."

Jessie wrapped both hands around the cold root beer bottle, holding it against his forehead for a moment to cool down before taking a sip. He needed a shower badly. His black curls were stuck to his forehead and all he could smell was dirt. "My choices are my own," he said finally, "except when they're not. What made you so sure I was going to choose you a second time?"

Bee smirked and leaned back in his seat. He pressed the bottle to his lips and tilted his head to take a long, dramatic swig before answering.

"Because you're selfish," Bee said on the tail of a satisfied swallow. "You're a selfish piece of shit and you weren't going to give up on what you want. Like I've said before, you could have anything you wanted—there is a lot that I can give you, but you're stuck on this one thing. You want to be 'complete', whatever that means to you, and you're not going to stall in the middle of the road. You weren't going to put everything on the line and throw it all away just to bring one soul back from the dead. You didn't feel *that* shitty about it."

"Hey," Jessie shot back in his defense, "I *did* consider it."

"Sure." Bee waved his hand dismissively. "But you didn't do it. Intention doesn't mean anything without action. I know I sound like I'm all words, but you know better than anyone that I will follow through with what I say. Every time."

The words fell heavily between them and lingered, a darker promise than they seemed. Jessie pressed his root beer bottle against his mouth and turned it around, slipping his tongue into the ridges.

"I'll make it up to you," Jessie ended up repeating himself.

"Yes, you will," Bee said.

"Tomorrow is Sunday." Jessie set the bottle down. "Are you going to stay the night?"

"I might as well," Bee said. "I think you and I have earned a late morning and a very alcoholic brunch."

"I would agree," Jessie said. "And after that, maybe…a game or two of blackjack?"

Bee smiled viciously, showing all his teeth. "You really are trying to butter me up, aren't you?"

"Is it working?" Jessie smiled back.

"Maybe," Bee said. "Maybe. What are we going to bet on? Anything interesting? You already put up your soul today, so that's no fun. We'll have to think of something else."

"I'm sure we can think of something more thrilling." Jessie rubbed the tip of his nose. "You could always bet your car."

"You would like that, wouldn't you?" Bee shook his head. "You can't even drive."

"Doesn't mean I won't take your car," Jessie said. "Unless you're afraid of losing."

"Like I said," Bee told him, "I always win more rounds than I lose."

"Then what are you afraid of?" Jessie challenged.

Bee lingered over his words for just a moment before he burst out laughing. His laughter was shrill and wild, like a barking fox.

"Absolutely nothing," the devil said. "Come on then, Jessie-beau. Let's get to bed."

A
THE DEVIL
WILL RETURN
A

ABOUT THE AUTHOR

Sirius is a lover of glory, gore, and monsters. They are a queer, nonbinary artist living in the hot and bothered South; currently residing in a little spot that has been dubbed 'Halloweentown', North Carolina. They are the writer of The Draonir Saga, the first book of which is Uncrowned (The Laughing Man House), and The Gentleman Demon Series, the first book of which is Swallow you Whole (Curious Corvid Publishing).

Sirius began writing at a young age and started exploring the publishing industry when they were thirteen. With many bumps along the way, they have learned a lot and grown in the craft that they would consider their one true love. Queer characters, gothic aesthetics, and royal drama (fantasy of manners) form the foundation of their storytelling.

When they are not writing, they work as a professional drag performer, weaving the characters from their stories into visual art for the stage.

NOTE FROM THE AUTHOR

It all started with Bonnie Tyler.

More specifically, it began with *Total Eclipse of the Heart'.*

My partner, Ellis, and I put together a drag routine that was based around "what if Dracula and Van Helsing fought to the death to an 80's power ballad?" You can fill in the rest. We took that act up and down the East Coast of North Carolina. At this point, I am pretty sure I could perform it in my sleep. We were hooked on the dynamic we created and it got better each time. And then at some point I looked at him in all seriousness and I asked, "what if Helsing was from Texas?"

I didn't mean to cut poor Quincy out of the narrative like that, but it was honestly funnier thinking about Helsing in a ten-gallon hat. The idea stuck, especially since I refused to drop the accent.

Dracula and Helsing have their own story that I have written. You will get to read that soon enough. It is a relevant piece of history, however, when it comes to Jessie's creation.

Because of Helsing (Abraham's) newfound history, I dove headfirst into country and folk horror and music. I'm a Southerner through and through, but I had always snubbed that part of me because it was not 'elegant' or 'academic'. Writing for Abraham gave me an excuse to embrace the part of me that had been latent for so long, just waiting for an excuse to spring to life.

The first story I wrote with the 'crossroads devil' was an epistolary horror short called *'Drawing from the Devil's Deck'*. As of this writing, it has yet to be published anywhere, but that is not really the point. It awoke something in me and I was, for lack of a better term, possessed. Soon after that I wrote *'Howling Devil in the Sticks'*, which was picked up and published in *'The Monster's Next Door'* anthology, edited by R.J. Carter. The story was the first time I ever wrote for 'Bee', and I could not let him go. Jessie had not come to me yet, but he was brewing.

Then it happened again, this time with *'The Devil Went Down to Georgia'*. My partner and I performed it for a crowd and it more or less cemented Jessie's fate. At that point, I was chomping at the bit to write for a young man who had sold his soul to the devil. A tale as old as time, and yet I could not let it go.

I wrote another short story called *'Slick as the Devil on Sunday'* for an anthology call. It was the first fully-blown erotic story I had written in a long time (for pleasure, anyway, and not for a ghostwriting gig). Jessie and Bee's fates were riveted together, at that point, and there was no prying them apart.

I wrote one more story, *'The Devil Comes at This Hour'*, which introduced Leslie. At that point, I had accumulated the lion's share of my cast. Jessie infected my brain in the same way Abraham had, granting me an outlet that I did not know I needed.

Blackjack + Moonshine is special to me in a way no other book has been in a long time. It was cathartic to write, and I poured my heart and soul into Jessie—the queer, neurodivergent Southern trans-man trapped in a Hell of his own creation. There are so many of my own experiences that went into the people (and devils) who surround him. I can honestly say that this novella is only the beginning. There is still much more of Jessie and Bee's story to be told.

After all, the devil is never satisfied, and he will always come back for more.

ACKNOWLEDGMENTS

I want to thank my partner, Janus, for all his hard work in making this book possible. From your tireless hours spent editing to your high tolerance for all the gross details. And I will never forget the moment you looked at me in all seriousness and asked, "so is Jessie where you store all your neurodivergence?" You were right. And I will give him a shower—eventually.

I want to thank my partner, Ellis, for not only giving me the inspiration but for supporting me endlessly. Thank you for fueling the fires of my country bumpkin heart, and for listening to all my dirty, dirty headcanons.

I also want to thank my dear friend Xavier for all the time you have put into taking Blackjack + Moonshine farther than I ever could have dreamed.

I want to thank Ravven White, Roxie Voorhees, Wendy Dalrymple, Red Lagoe, and Rae Knowles for being the very first to give this book a shot. Thank you for all your kind words and encouragement, it really has meant the world to me.

SLICK AS THE DEVIL ON SUNDAY

A SHORT STORY

A mile-long dirt road with more curves than a hatbox ribbon was all that separated the old white church from Jessie Livingston's house. He did not mind the walk, not even in the middle of a humid Southern spring. The road was slightly damp and the sharp smell of ragweed tickled his throat, but his wide-brimmed hat kept the sun off his nose, and he draped his grey suit jacket over his arm to keep the sweat off his collar. Treacherous pits and puddles threatened to disgrace his already worn-through shoes, and he was just distracted enough that he nearly stumbled twice.

The sermon was the farthest thing from his mind. It was all fire and brimstone—what else was there? He had been distracted by the preacher's shiny new watch and the way he kept clearing his throat before stomping his feet on the ground. That man was loud, boorish, and red-faced in a way that when his bald head began to sweat, he glistened like a candy apple at the fair.

Jessie's stomach growled. Had he eaten any breakfast?

Going to church was one thing, listening and learning something was another. He already had one bid for his soul, and he was not looking to set up an auction. If anything, a 9AM service was just a way to kill time on a Sunday. A *safe* way.

Jessie turned down his neighborhood street. The roads were paved, there, thank whoever. His aching feet screamed with relief at the change to even ground. He made another turn to head down the shaded little street that ended in a cul-de-sac. There were a few houses on either side, some more evenly separated than others. His was shrouded behind two willow trees and buried underneath a wall of pink azalea bushes that were doing their best to consume his front porch. If nature was trying to reclaim the damn thing, he was willing to let it go.

Jessie squinted, trying to get a better view of his porch as he pulled up his suit jacket for his keys. There was nothing out of place that he could see. The rocking chair was still, the screen door looked undisturbed. The green and brown glass bottles hanging from the roof clinked their sides together in the sluggish breeze, but nothing was broken or out of place.

'Maybe he isn't here,' some part of him knew that it wasn't true, but he held onto that hope for as long as it took him to walk up the front steps and open the screen door.

"Good morning, Jessie," the familiar voice startled him so badly that Jessie dropped his keys. He bent to pick them up, his fingers trembling a little as he searched the ring for the correct one. The screen door swung into his backside, shuddering with the sudden stop.

"Shit," he muttered. He straightened and pushed loose black curls out of his face, knocking his hat off completely in the process. *"Fuck."*

"Do you need some help?" the porch creaked underneath the weight of an additional shoe. Jessie's heart felt like it was being squeezed.

"I've got it," he said sharply, "thanks." He looked over at person standing on his steps. Well, not a *person,* really. Bee was less human than he looked, but he played the part very well. He dressed like a televangelist—all in white like it was Easter, except for the blood red dress shirt that he kept unbuttoned at the top. He had a jeweled ring on every finger, and his bluebonnet eyes smiled behind round purple sunglasses. He held up a flat brown box and Jessie caught the faint, tooth-achingly sweet scent of maple.

"Maple donuts," Bee said, "I know that you skipped breakfast."

Jessie's mouth went dry. His tongue felt gummy as he swiped it around the inside of his cheeks. "There was a woman at church who made biscuits. I ate."

"Liar," Bee winked. He closed the distance between them in two quick steps. Up close, he was taller than Jessie, and his skin smelled like clove oil and burnt tobacco. He emanated heat, like standing next to a brazier, and his dark hair gleamed with slick pomade that held every strand in place. Standing so close to him made Jessie's heart beat even faster, and it suddenly became very difficult to swallow.

Bee reached out and wrapped his fingers around the bent doorknob, sliding his thumb into the brass ding and stroking it back and forth. He eyes lingered over Jessie and he grinned, flashing a mouthful of unsettlingly white teeth.

"We can keep playing this game," Bee lowered his voice so that the words throbbed intimately in the air between them, "if you'd like."

"What game?" Jessie breathed.

Bee turned the knob, even though it was still locked, and the door sprang open. He kept it cracked, just enough for a cool rush of air conditioning to hit Jessie in the face. Jessie hadn't realized how much he was sweating until that moment.

"Keep lying to me," Bee said. "Why did you go to church this morning?"

"I was avoiding you," Jessie said through his teeth.

"That isn't a lie," Bee clucked his tongue.

"No," Jessie admitted. He tried to push past Bee to get through the door, but he was stopped by the edge of the donut box.

"I think you are forgetting the vital part of our bargain," Bee's normal, patient tone was starting to sound a little thin. "It is *body* and soul."

Jessie *really* could not swallow. He turned his head and spat onto the porch, resting his hand against his chest as if that could stop his heart from quivering. "I didn't forget."

"You came to me, first, at the crossroad outside of that little church."

"I remember," Jessie ground his teeth.

"And you said *'anything.'*"

Jessie pulled in a deep breath through his nose and met Bee's eyes. He tried not to, when he could avoid it—Bee's eyes had an effect like morphine. They made him feel numb. If Jessie stared into them for too long, his fingers and toes would start to tingle. He swiped his tongue over his cheeks again—only this time to try and banish the sort of cold numbness that was starting to take over the organ.

"Right," Jessie said, "and I meant it. I signed the contract. It is only...one Sunday. Shit." He brought up his hand to rub his face. "Have some pity."

Bee laughed. It was a short, sharp sound without any real mirth behind it. He finally released the knob and let the door spring open. The sudden rush of cold, damp air made Jessie want to throw up.

"Pity, I don't have," Bee said. "It is your bargain, Jessie, these are *your* terms."

Jessie felt no relief stepping over the threshold. If anything, his stomach felt like a ball of ice, and his hands shook as he threw his suit coat down over a chair. He made his way towards the kitchen, hoping for a cup of coffee or—maybe even some whiskey for his nerves. He unbuttoned his sleeves and rolled them up to his elbow, raking his fingers through his curls again as if he could fidget away his distress.

Bee set the box of donuts down on the table. The last thing Jessie ever wanted to do again was eat.

"The kitchen?" Bee asked.

Jessie shook his head. "The bedroom," he said. "I just want some water first."

"Dealer's choice," Bee shrugged and loosened a few more buttons on his shirt. "It makes no difference to me."

There was a glass of water on the counter leftover from that morning, but Jessie didn't trust it. He poured it out in the sink and refilled the glass fresh from the spigot, but it was hard to take even a moment when he could feel Bee's eyes drilling into the back of his skull the entire time.

He gave up and carried the glass to the bedroom. He couldn't hear Bee's footsteps, but he knew that he was being followed.

Early afternoon shadows swallowed up every corner of the bedroom. Between the trees, the covered porch, and the faint yellow curtains—the only light that could make it through was weak and pale, barely enough to lend even the softest glow to the intimate scene. Jessie took a big gulp of water and set his glass down on the bedside table, exhaling sharply and flicking his tongue over his teeth. His hands were still trembling so badly that he could barely get a grip on his vest buttons to push them through the holes.

"You are so nervous," Bee's voice skated by his ear, so close that he could feel warm breath against his neck. "Why? You have done it all before. A dozen times, at least."

"I don't know," Jessie clenched his jaw. "Maybe it is because you make me nervous."

"You should know better than to admit that," Bee moved closer to the bed. He reached out and placed his hand against the white metal frame, stroking his thumb over the bare black spots where the paint had flaked away. "One would think you would use at least part of your Faustian bargain for a better bed. One that doesn't look like it came from your grandmother."

Jessie threw his vest onto the floor. "Can't you pull one out of thin air?" His words had a sarcastic bite as he tore off his shirt. "Couldn't you flip over one of your cards and snap your fingers or something like that?"

"Maybe," Bee said. "You haven't asked for it."

"I don't need it. Who am I trying to impress?" Jessie hesitated at unbuttoning his slacks, taking just a few seconds longer to slide them down his hips. Bee was still fully dressed, only his shirt was slightly more unbuttoned than before, and just enough to offer a peek at the forest of dark hair across his chest.

Jessie bit his bottom lip. "How do you want me?"

Bee pressed his hand down against the bed until the springs in the old mattress creaked. "All fours," he said, "you can put your head down this time."

The springs dug into Jessie's knees as he mounted the bed. The quilted cover did not offer much padding, but he still managed to adjust himself somewhat comfortably. He put his head down, resting his cheek against a cool, lumpy pillow. As many times as he had done this, he still could not calm his racing heart. Even with his head down, he felt dizzy—like the walls were sliding towards him, threatening to cave in.

"I am going to pass out," he said.

"No," Bee told him, "You won't." His hands were almost too hot to bear. He slid them over the curve of Jessie's bare ass, scraping blunt fingernails down his thighs. "Besides, you are the one who refuses to stay on your back."

"I don't like looking in your eyes," Jessie admitted. Bee flattened his hands against Jessie's thighs, spreading them wider apart until everything was exposed. Jessie curled his fingers into the quilt underneath him, gripping it tightly as he felt Bee's fingers start to explore the warm space between his legs.

Jessie hated himself for how wet he was, already. Maybe it was the anticipation, or simply his body's response to fear. Bee's fingertips lingered over his open entrance, gathering up enough lubrication to slide up to his clit and stroke it slowly. Jessie turned his face to moan into his pillow, his thighs already quivering with the exertion of holding him up.

"You are the devil," Jessie groaned, muffled by the pillow.

"Tiresome that you should say it, but yes," Bee said. He teased Jessie's entrance again, sliding in just one finger at first, going down to the second knuckle. A second finger joined in, and he pushed them as deep as they could go, twisting his hand and grinding his knuckles against Jessie's slick cunt.

"Which one?" Jessie gasped.

"Patience," Bee thrust his fingers in, deeper, spreading them apart and stretching Jessie open. "I will gag you."

Heat surged up to Jessie's face and made spots float across his vision. He swallowed another moan, biting his tongue to keep the hard, needy sounds in check. Another second passed and Bee withdrew his fingers, smacking his open hand against Jessie's soaked entrance.

Those hot, wicked fingertips traveled their way up—prodding between Jessie's ass cheeks and teasing the second hole. Jessie sucked in a breath, his entire body tensing until every angry muscle was painfully tight. Bee paused, there, keeping his fingers completely still, but applying enough pressure that Jessie had already started to open up for him.

"Fuck," Jessie huffed, "what are you waiting for--?"

Before he could register what was happening, Bee grabbed hold of his hips. For a split second, Jessie was in the air, and then his back collided with the bed as he was flipped over. The springs dug into his spine, and he yelped in protest. He kicked his legs out and Bee grabbed them, pulling them back down towards the bed while keeping them wide apart.

"What the hell!" Jessie yelled.

"Yes," Bee slid his sunglasses down his nose before pulling them off entirely. "You get the idea." He set the glasses down on the bedside table, right next to Jessie's waterglass, and went back to holding down his legs. "I want you to look at me, Jessie."

Jessie refused. He kept his eyes fixed at the popcorn ceiling, gripping the quilt underneath him hard enough that his knuckles turned white.

"Jessie," Bee's voice dropped to an impossible low, resonate and dark, and it echoed off the bedroom walls. "*Look at me.*"

It was a command that did not invite disobedience. Jessie felt compelled to do as he was told, even though every part of his remaining free will clawed against it. He pulled his eyes away from the ceiling and found Bee's gaze. Those uncanny bluebonnet irises with pupils like drops of ink that seemed to get wider and wider, as if they could pull Jessie into their depths and swallow him up completely.

Every muscle in Jessie's body began to relax as if he had just swallowed a handful of pills. His lips parted and his jaw slackened, but no sound came out.

"Better," Bee smiled, "so much better." He dragged his nails up Jessie's thighs again, although this time the sensation was heightened tenfold. Jessie tried to moan, but it came out as a gurgling sound. Even when Bee lowered his head, Jessie was stuck on those blue eyes. Blue was all he could see, now. Everything in the room looked washed in cold cerulean.

Jessie wanted to ask if Bee was going to take off his rings, but even if he could, he already knew the answer.

Bee's fingers were still slick when he placed them against Jessie's second hole once more. There was no coaxing, this time, or warning. He shoved two of them inside, pushing them down to the third knuckle and grinding his hand against Jessie's ass. Jessie gargled again, trying to cry out—but all he got was spittle dripping out the sides of his mouth. He could not move. He could hardly breathe. Everything felt slow, surreal, and like there was a great big slab of cement sitting on his chest.

The sharp jewels on Bee's rings sliced open his skin. The pain was like a knife being dragged across his sphincter. Jessie could feel his own hot blood pouring around Bee's fingers, but that only seemed to encourage him. A third finger joined, and then a fourth. Bee worked them back and forth, coating them with Jessie's blood, twisting and bending them until the tight ring of muscle had relaxed enough to let his whole hand through. He worked it up to the thumb, and Jessie tried to grip the quilt underneath him again, but his hands were too weak. He tried to close his eyes, but as heavy as they felt, they would not shut. It was like being dead, but even death would have been a mercy. If the devil's gaze had numbed him through and through, that would be another matter altogether. But every stroke, every cut, every twist and every thrust was heightened. Jessie felt like Bee was reaching for his innards, like he was going to rip his bowels out through his asshole.

Bee's entire hand was inside of him, clenching into a tight fist. Jessie could feel every knuckle, every ring, twisting and thrusting and filling him up entirely.

"Very good," Bee praised him, "I wonder how much of my arm I could get inside before I ripped you in half."

Terror ripped through Jessie. He could not tell if Bee meant it. Bee's fingers teased his clit again, stroking it as he thrust his other hand inside of him. Even the softest touch against Jessie's clit made it feel like it was on fire. He hated himself for how good it felt, and how much he wanted to orgasm. He knew that Bee wanted him to beg for it, too, although he did not know how he could when his tongue was like lead in his mouth.

"There it is," Bee said, and his fingers began to move quicker—making circles around the head of Jessie's clit. "Just there. I can feel it. I bet you can, too." Faster and faster. His fingers were unrelenting, merciless. Jessie wanted to scream.

And then, just like that, it was all over. Bee withdrew his hands. He pulled his fingers away from Jessie's clit and he slid his hand out of his ass at the same time. His rings snagged again, and Jessie cried out in pain. He could speak again, at least, but now his throat felt raw. His whole chest felt caved in and his lungs felt as though they were on fire. He rolled over onto his side. He ached between his thighs, pleasure attempting to override pain, but in the end it all ached. There was blood on his thighs, and blood soaking through the quilt underneath him. His entire body shivered—a comedown from a high that left him feeling like he was going to vomit.

"...Please," was the first word out of Jessie's mouth. Bee licked the blood from his own fingers, cocking one dark brow as if he had not heard correctly.

"Please?" Bee echoed back. The devil was already sliding off the bed. Jessie reached out, grabbing hold of his white suit jacket and smearing red blood all over the expensive fabric.

"Please!" Jessie ground his teeth. "I want to, I need to…"

"Need to?" Bee grabbed his hand, crushing Jessie's fingers in his iron grip. "Maybe next time, you will let me in when I come calling, and not waste time shuffling your feet through mildewing pews."

"Is that what this is?" Jessie demanded, his anger overriding the fact that he still felt like he could not catch his breath. "You are angry that I went to church?"

"No," Bee said patiently, "but you of all people should know—I operate on a tight schedule. And if you cannot take that seriously, I am afraid we can't move forward doing business together. And I think that I have done very well by you with our bargain. Don't you agree?"

He was right. The transformation had come in thin, almost transparent layers—but Jessie was seeing the changes every day. Small things. His sideburns were growing out. His chest had started to shrink into non-existence. His voice had dropped several octaves, to the point where he even sang a hymn—and was happy with the result.

"You said," Bee told him, "Body and soul. Whatever it takes."

"Right," Jessie wiped at his mouth. He dropped his eyes again. He still felt dizzy, but at least the world was back to yellow. Yellow, not blue—although he still did not trust his limbs. "I will respect your time."

"You will," Bee said as he picked up his sunglasses and slipped them back on. "Eat something, too. I left the donuts on the table."

"You're a bastard," Jessie muttered.

"And I'm your problem," Bee said, "for eternity." He tilted his head and flashed a grin. "I will check on you tomorrow. If you need me, I'm just next door." He grasped Jessie's chin, tilting it up so that their eyes would have met if the colored sunglasses did not obscure them so well. "Keep lying to me, Jessie, you know I think it brings out the best in you."

He dropped Jessie's chin, and then he was gone. The smell of cloves and tobacco lingered after, barely covered by the sharp, rusty scent of blood.